Chapter One

JAX

PRESENT DAY

"What's all this for?" I step into the condo I share with my longtime girlfriend, Willow, and find rose petals and candles scattered all over the place. When I glance at our coffee table, two champagne flutes are sitting on top with a bucket of ice and a bottle of champagne next to it. I was only gone for a couple hours, having a beer with my brother, Jase.

Willow steps forward, and her lips curl into a shy smile, a look I rarely see on her face. My girlfriend isn't shy by any means. With her midnight black hair that has different colors running through it—this month it's blue, that same blue that matches her eyes—tattoos covering most of her arms, perky tits, and tanned, toned legs for days, she's sexy as fuck. And with her *I don't give a fuck* attitude, she's sassy as hell. With her heart that beats outside of her chest, she's giving and loving and selfless. But she isn't shy. So when she hits me with that rare smile, I know something is up.

"Today is our ten-year anniversary," she tells me, her shy smile splitting into a wide grin. I give her a shocked look. Not because I don't know what today is, but because Willow Montgomery doesn't celebrate anniversaries. So the fact that she's standing before me, suddenly celebrating our anniversary, definitely has my interest piqued.

"It is," I agree. "An entire decade of getting to spend every day with you."

Willow's eyes fill with tears, and my thoughts jump to a worst-case scenario. "Baby, what's wrong?" Whatever it is, we'll deal with it together. My girlfriend may live for today, but she knows I'm always going to be right by her side, living for today with her.

"Nothing is wrong," she says, taking another step forward. "I'm just...I'm kind of nervous."

Pulling her into my arms, I plant a kiss on her forehead. She smells like the lotion she puts on every morning after she gets out of the shower. Light Blue by Dolce & Gabbana. It's sweet and feminine and I could recognize the scent anywhere. "You're going to have to help me out here," I murmur. "You were just smiling and now you're in tears."

Willow pulls back and wipes the tears from her eyes. "Jax, you are everything to me. You aren't just my boyfriend, you're my best friend, my other half."

My heart pounds against my ribcage with every word she speaks. "I feel the same way."

She pulls something out of the front pocket of her jeans. A ring... No, not *a* ring. Two rings. "I'm ready, Jax," she says through her watery smile. "I'm ready to marry you. To spend the rest of my life as your wife. Jaxson Crawford, will you marry me?"

My gaze flits between Willow's hope-filled eyes and the two rings she's holding. The one I bought for her ten years ago, and a simple silver band that I'm assuming is meant for me. I want so badly to say yes, but before I do, I need to know one thing. "What's changed your mind?"

Smiling, Willow places the rings on the coffee table and grabs a small, square black book. "This."

She hands it to me, and I turn to the first page and then the second and then the third. Each page is filled with pictures of us, of our life, starting with the first night she took pity on me and took me out with her.

Chapter Two
JAX
TEN YEARS AGO

"I'M OUT, BRO," JASE, MY YOUNGER BROTHER, says, popping his head into my workstation. While I'm waiting for my last appointment of the day to arrive, I'm working on a sketch for another client.

"Already?" I glance over at the clock and see it's only six o'clock.

"Promised Celeste and Sky I would pick up dinner and bring it to them. They're getting ready for that fashion show coming up. You want to come over for dinner?"

He asks the same question every day, and every day I tell him the same thing. "I'm good, bro. Go be with your family."

For as far back as I can remember, Jase, our sister Quinn, and I have lived together. Whether it was in North Carolina where we grew up, or here in New York, where we've been living for the last several years. We've always stuck together. Until recently, when both my siblings moved out and in with their significant others. It's weird living on my own. I'm almost forty years old and I've never had a place to myself. I imagined the townhouse would become a bachelor pad. I would throw parties every night and have women over without having to worry about the innocent ears of my niece hearing anything. But after a couple months, the partying got old, and the mindless sex got even older.

As much as I would love to spend time with Jase or Quinn, I don't want to impose. They moved out for a reason. To start their own lives. It's not like I don't see them every day. Quinn helps out occasionally by running the front desk at the tattoo shop Jase and I own: Forbidden Ink. And since I work with Jase at said tattoo shop, I see him every day.

"You sure?" he asks.

"Yeah, man. I'm going to head home after my appointment and get some shut eye. Late night, last night." Late night watching reruns of Breaking Bad on Netflix...

"All right, well, if you change your mind..."

"Yeah, yeah, I know. Get out of here, and make sure

you give my favorite niece a kiss."

"She's your only niece," Jase volleys.

"For now." I laugh. Celeste recently found out she's pregnant and they're expecting twins. Nobody knows the sexes yet.

A little while later, my client shows up. She's a twenty-five-year-old breast cancer survivor and gets a pink ribbon with a quote down the side of her ribcage. By the time I finish and clean up, it's just after eight o'clock.

Gage, a tattooist who works here, and Evan, who answers the phones while apprenticing with us, stop by to let me know they're leaving for the night.

When I unplug my phone from the dock and switch off my music, I hear the soft sound of pop music playing somewhere. Willow must still be here. She's the only one of us who listens to that girly shit.

Walking down the hall, I check her workstation, but it's empty. I follow the music, until I find where it's coming from. The bathroom.

As I raise my fist to knock on the door, her voice rises several octaves as she sings completely out of tune with the singer. The horrible sound has me laughing out loud.

"Hey, Beyoncé." I bang on the door. "I think you're late for your performance."

I'm still laughing when the door swings open and Willow steps out, dressed in a pair of skintight dark blue jeans with more holes up and down her legs than there is material, and a blood red shirt that covers her tits, but exposes her entire midriff, showing off her pierced belly button. Her black hair is straight and bits of hot pink peak out from underneath.

She's only been working here for a short time, but I've never seen her dressed in anything but our business shirts, which cover her completely, and regular jeans or shorts.

"Like what you see?" She winks dramatically. My eyes meet hers, and I can't help but stare at the gorgeous woman in front of me. Her face is usually free of makeup, and she always looks pretty, but with whatever she's done to her eyes and lips, she looks fucking hot as hell. And older. That's the problem. The makeup and clothes make her look older.

"Playing dress up?" I joke, trying to play off how attracted I suddenly am to her.

"Funny." She rolls her eyes. "Can you do me a favor and button the back of my top?" She turns around and lifts her silky hair, exposing her slim neck and artfully tattooed back. I step toward her and quickly button the couple of buttons she couldn't reach, making sure not to touch her in any way.

"Thanks." She turns back around, hitting me with a bright smile. "So, what are you up to tonight?"

She sits on the couch and grabs the tallest pair of black fuck-me heels I've ever seen, slipping each one onto her slender feet. Jesus, I need to stop eye-fucking her. She's ten years younger than me and I'm her boss.

"Jax?" she prompts. Shit, she asked me a question.

"Umm... just going to watch Netflix." I flinch as the words come out. Can I sound any more like a loser?

She laughs. "It's Friday night and you're a single guy. Netflix is for teenagers who need an excuse to make out, or old people who have nothing better to do with their time."

"I am old," I say dryly, which causes her to laugh harder.

"What are you, like thirty-five? That's hardly old." She sets her foot down and stands.

"Thirty-seven," I correct her. "And I've done my fair share of partying. I guess I'm just over that scene."

"Have you ever been to Flora's?" She steps towards me, so close I can smell her perfume. It's sweet and soft. Delicate.

"Jax." She smirks, knowing I'm all caught up in how she looks and smells. "Flora's?"

"No." I shake my head. "Never heard of it."

"Come with me tonight."

"Ehh..."

"Come on." She smacks my bicep playfully. "You're too young to be home on a Friday night... or any night for that matter. Life's too short." She hits me with her pearly-white smile. "Please."

I don't think it would matter what she's asking me for. Dressed like that, smelling like that, smiling like that. I would say yes to anything she asks.

"Sure. I think I have an extra shirt in the office."

Chapter Three

JAX

WE GET TO THE CLUB AND WILLOW SEEMS TO know everyone. She doesn't wait in the long as hell line like everyone else, and the bouncer not only lets us in, but tells her to head up to the VIP section. When we get to the roped off area, there are about two dozen people drinking and dancing. They greet Willow, all wanting to hug her and offer her a drink. I watch quietly as she laughs and flirts with everyone who approaches her. She doesn't do it in a tease sort of way, but more of a friendly, she just loves everyone sort of way.

She introduces me to everyone as her friend, then hands me a shot. "To today!" she yells over the music.

"To today," I agree. We both down our shots and then

she hands me another and then another. Her friends join in, and we spend the next however long drinking and laughing. Willow does most of the talking and I find myself just listening. Soaking in every word she speaks. She talks about work, the different customers she had. About visiting the Farmer's Market this weekend. One of her friends complains about a co-worker and Willow tells her not to stress. Life is too short.

When she catches me watching her, she asks, "What?"

"Nothing. I'm just enjoying learning about you," I tell her honestly. She's the most care-free person I've ever met.

"And what did you learn?" she asks.

"You like to have fun."

She smiles. "We only have one life, Jax. We have to make it count."

After downing another shot, she pulls her phone out and insists we take a selfie together. Then she grabs my hand and guides me onto the dance floor.

"I love this song." She smiles wide and wraps her arms around my neck. I'm not sure what this song is or who sings it, but neither matters as Willow separates her thighs and grinds down on my leg. My hands find the curves of her hips as she shimmies up and down to the beat of the music.

She throws her head back, and her fingers tighten around my neck to hold her up. My eyes go straight to her slender throat, and my only thought is what her skin would taste like. It's glistening from the hot club and the dancing and drinking, and I wonder if I licked down her throat if it would taste salty, or if it would taste sweet like she smells. *Probably a mixture of both.*

But before I can find out, Willow's head snaps up and her blue eyes meet mine. Her lips curl into a beautiful smile before she turns her body around, giving me her back. Without missing a beat, her arms go over her head and she shakes her ass. Briefly, I wonder if she has any idea that I'm not dancing, but instead standing here like a horny teenager, watching the show.

Willow backs her ass up and hits my crotch, and it's then I realize I'm sporting a semi. Fuck, there's no way she didn't feel that. Her face turns slightly so our eyes meet once again, and she hits me with the sexiest smirk, telling me she definitely felt it.

She backs up until our bodies are flush and then she grinds her ass against the bulge in my pants. Her arm comes up and hooks around my nape, and she pulls my face forward. Her soft lips find my ear, and she murmurs, "Let's take this elsewhere."

Jesus, fuck. I want to say yes, but I can't. It's one thing to drink and dance with her. It's another thing to fuck her.

"Don't do that," she says. She turns back around, so our mouths are only inches apart. "Don't overthink this."

"I'm your—" I attempt to argue, but her tongue darts out and traces my bottom lip, effectively shutting me up. Her tongue then moves to my top lip before it slips past my parted lips. Stroking, teasing, caressing. Our kiss deepens. My hands find her ass, and then I'm lifting her into the air.

"Bathroom," she murmurs across my mouth.

I do as she says as she continues to kiss me with abandon.

I don't think about how crowded this place is, or who's watching us. I don't consider how many people will be in said bathroom, or how this is going to work. I'm too lost in Willow and her kisses and touches.

When we get to the bathroom, there are a couple of women, but neither of us pay any attention to them. We enter the handicap stall and Willow drops to her feet. She unbuttons her pants and pushes them, along with her underwear, down.

My mind is telling me this is wrong, that I should stop this. At least take her home and do this on a bed, but Willow's voice pushes my thoughts away when she turns around, slaps her hands against the bathroom stall wall, and says, "Fuck me, Jax. Please."

I unzip my pants and pull my hard cock out, stroking it a few times. Willow's luscious ass is perked up in the air, and she shakes it back and forth, silently begging me to take her.

"Willow, are you sure?" I hate that I'm being such a downer here but fuck, I'm in over my head with this woman. People talk about hooking up in bathrooms, but I've never seen or done it. My alcohol-filled brain is telling me to do it, but the adult in me is telling me this is irresponsible as hell and I'm going to regret it when the alcohol is out of my system.

"Jax, now," Willow growls, pushing the responsible part of my brain aside.

As I'm lining up the head of my cock with her entrance, there's a knock on the door. "Hurry up! I need to go pee!" a woman screeches. And just like that, the moment is gone. I pull back and Willow turns around with the most adorable pout on her lips.

"Jax." Her brows furrow as she watches me tuck my rock-hard dick into my pants the best I can.

"I can't do this," I tell her. "Not here...not like this." I step towards her and bend at the waist so I can pull her pants up. She swats my hands away and finishes herself.

"Come home with me," I whisper against her ear.

She glances up at me and shakes her head. "No, I don't know what I was thinking." She closes her eyes.

"Willow." When I say her name, her eyes flutter back open. "I'm sorry..."

"You have nothing to apologize for." She plasters on a fake smile. "You're my boss and it would've been a mistake."

I nod in agreement, but my insides are tightening in disagreement. "Why don't I walk you home?"

She shakes her head. "That's okay. I'm a big girl." She winks, but it's not carefree like before.

We exit the stall, and a couple of women gape at us, thinking we just hooked up in there.

Instead of going back up to the VIP area, Willow heads to the exit, and I follow.

"Please let me walk you home," I insist. I'm not sure where she lives, but it's late, and nowhere in New York is really safe at this time.

"Jax, really. I'm fine." Her voice is rough in frustration.

As much as it kills me to let her walk away, I don't want to piss her off, so I tell her okay and that I'll see her tomorrow at work.

And then I watch her walk down the street, wait a minute so she doesn't know I'm following her, and then head in the same direction. She walks fast as hell, especially for a woman who's been drinking and is walking in tall as hell heels, but I easily keep up. Making sure to remain far enough back, so she won't see me, I follow her several blocks. When she stops at a quickie mart, I hide in the shadows. A few minutes later, she comes out with a large duffel bag over her shoulder and continues on her way.

She walks a few more blocks and then she stops in front of an abandoned building. Pulling a blanket out of the duffel bag, she shakes it out, spreads it out in front of her, and then drops down onto it. She fluffs the bag to use it as a pillow, then lays her head on it.

What the fuck is going on? I wait for her to jump up and tell me she knows I've been following her. Tell me she's joking and laugh in my face. But she doesn't. Her eyes close and her breathing evens out. As I watch her sleep, it hits me that Willow is homeless.

When I met her, she was drawing pictures in Central Park along the bridge. She was dressed in a ripped T-shirt and jean shorts, and I could see a couple of tattoos peeking out. She was laughing with a couple who were checking out her artwork, and I was immediately drawn to her. I could tell right away she was talented and knew she would make a great addition to the shop. When I asked if she could tattoo, she told me she would love to learn, so I taught her. She caught on quickly and has been working at Forbidden Ink ever since. So, I know she makes enough money to survive. To live in an apartment.

She mentioned a while back that she and her boyfriend broke up, but I didn't think much of it. Is it possible he kicked her out? But then why wouldn't she just get another place? It doesn't make any sense.

Well, whatever the story is, there's no way I'm going to let her sleep out here all night. Not wanting to startle her, I call out her name. She squirms but doesn't wake up, obviously already in a deep sleep.

"Willow, wake up," I say louder. This time her eyes open. It takes her a second, but once she realizes she isn't dreaming, her body pops up and she looks around.

"Let's go," I tell her before she can even think of an excuse or a lie to feed me.

She considers arguing, I can see it in her eyes, but she must realize I'm not playing around, because she lets out a deep sigh, shoves her blanket into her duffle bag, and then stands.

Chapter Four
WILLOW

WHILE WE WALK TO THE SUBWAY STATION, JAX doesn't say a word, and I greatly appreciate it. I've already made enough of an ass of myself for one night. When we get on the subway, he continues with his silent treatment, but the longer he doesn't talk, the more I just want to get the conversation over with. Like ripping the band-aid off. Why prolong it? We get off in Cobble Hill and walk a couple blocks through a small suburbia neighborhood lined with cute brick townhouses.

When we arrive at his place, he unlocks the door and holds it open for me to walk through first. It's fall in New York, so the temperatures tend to fluctuate. This week has been on the cooler side, but when I step into Jax's house, it's nice and warm. I take a look around and find the place to be neat and tidy. The furniture is nice, nothing fancy, but it's all good quality.

"The bedrooms and bathrooms are upstairs," he says, walking toward the stairs. I follow him up and he stops at the first door. "This is the guest bedroom and it has its own bathroom. It's stocked with toiletries and towels are under the sink."

He steps back to walk away, but I stop him. "Don't you want to talk about it?" After thinking about it, I'm going with ripping the band-aid off.

"About what? The fact that I almost fucked my employee in the bathroom of a club? My employee who is over ten years younger than me." His eyes shoot to the ceiling like he's praying to God to help him before he looks back down at me. "Or the fact that you've been living on the streets for God knows how long and haven't said a word to any of us?"

"All of the above." I shrug, unsure what to say.

"I'm tired, still half-buzzed, and it's late..." He glances at his cell phone. "Or I guess early since it's almost four in the morning. We have to be at the shop in a few hours, so how about we shower, get some sleep, and we can talk in the morning."

"Okay." I give him a half-smile, hoping to knock his evident frustration down a few notches. "I'll see you in the morning—er, in a few hours."

Closing the door behind me, I strip out of my clothes

and head straight for the shower. It's been a few months since I've had a shower that's not in a women's shelter, and I find myself relaxing under the hot spray until the water goes cold. Hopefully Jax already finished his shower. I grab a fluffy towel and dry off, then grab my pajamas to change into.

Since I have a couple hours before we leave, I wonder if Jax would mind if I do a load of laundry. I can do it at the laundry mat, but they're freaking gross. Tiptoeing over to the room I saw him go into, I knock lightly in case he's already asleep. If he is, I'll just find the washer and dryer and do a load before he wakes up. I doubt he'll even notice.

"Come in," he calls out. My hand grasps the knob to open the door when he pulls the door at the same time. My body stumbles forward, and just before I think I'm going to faceplant, Jax catches me in his strong arms.

"Jesus, you okay?" He chuckles, the sound reverberating through my body and going straight to the apex of my thighs.

"Yeah." I laugh softly. "I didn't realize you were opening the door."

"Everything okay?" He looks me up and down.

"Yeah, I was just wondering if you would mind if I used your washer and dryer to do a load. I'll have it done before we leave in the morning."

Jax's jaw ticks and I worry I've overstepped. He's already been kind enough to offer me a bed and a shower.

NIKKI ASH

"You know what... never mind..." I turn to leave when he grabs my wrist, twirling me back around.

"Are you homeless?" he asks, even though he already knows the answer.

"Yes."

"For how long?"

"For about a year now."

"Fuck," he curses under his breath. "Why haven't you said anything?"

"You're my employer. It's not your problem."

"I'm also your friend." His eyes bore into mine.

"Not really," I say honestly. I've never been one to beat around the bush. "I mean you're nice and I love working for you, but we aren't friends."

When his brows furrow, I add, "Where did I live before I became homeless?" When he doesn't answer, I continue. "What's my favorite color? My favorite food? Where am I from? What's my ex-boyfriend's name?"

Jax's shoulders slump, and I give him a reassuring smile. "I'm not saying all that to blame you. I'm just explaining that we aren't friends. I used to have friends... when I lived in Michigan, where I was born and raised. Then I met Henry, and after dating for a few months, he got a promotion and was transferred to New York, so I moved with him. The friends I made here were all his, and when we broke up, they remained his."

"Why didn't you move back home?"

"Both of my parents died from cancer. My mom from

breast cancer, and a few years later, my dad from colon cancer."

"What about all those people at the club?"

"Those aren't friends. They're acquaintances. I don't do friends, Jax." Stepping out of his grip, I head back down the hallway to grab my dirty clothes. "Is the washer upstairs?"

"Down," he says. I jump when his voice comes out right behind me.

"You can go to sleep."

"Thanks for letting me know," he replies dryly, following me down the stairs.

After I throw my clothes in, along with some detergent, I close the lid, then go straight to the kitchen to get a glass of water. When I can't find the cups, Jax opens the correct cabinet and hands me a glass.

"Thanks."

"Why are you homeless?" he asks, settling his back against the edge of the counter.

Not wanting his pity, I consider lying to him, but something tells me he's not going to stop until he gets the truth out of me. He already stalked my ass 'home.'

"Long story short, a year ago, the gynecologist found cancer cells in my uterus. I could've gone through chemo and all that, but instead I chose to get a hysterectomy. Henry didn't agree with it because it meant we could never have kids. When I told him kids were no longer in my plan, and neither was marriage, he dumped me. Since the apartment was his, I had to leave."

Jax's eyes go wide, and his arms which are crossed over his chest, flex. "When you said you needed a couple weeks off to go on vacation you were having fucking major surgery?"

I nod.

"My insurance covered a portion of it, but not all, and then there were follow up visits and radiation and the medications. Unlike the hospital which allows you to make payments, the private facilities require payment at the time of visit."

"Jesus, Willow." Jax sighs. "You should've said something. Are you okay now?"

"I am. I'm done with all the treatments and as of right now, I'm cancer free. I'm saving for a place now."

Jax stares at me for several beats before he says, "You're staying here."

"Tonight?" I ask, confused.

"No, indefinitely." I open my mouth to argue, but he shakes his head. "I have a three-bedroom, three-bathroom place to myself. I'm not taking no for an answer." He lifts a brow, daring me to argue.

"Okay, on two conditions."

"You're giving me conditions when I'm offering you my home to live in for free." He throws his head back in a laugh, and I find myself smiling at how sexy he looks when he laughs.

"My first condition..." I raise my voice so he can hear

me over his laughter, and he stops. "My first condition is I pay for half of the bills."

Jax is already shaking his head. "Not happening. Next condition."

I huff in frustration. "My other condition is that you're not allowed to get attached to me. It's inevitable we'll hook up, and I have no doubt it will be hot as hell, but that's all it can ever be. No friendship, no relationship."

Jax stares at me for several seconds before he busts out laughing again. "Are you serious right now?"

"Yes, very." I give him a dry look, so he knows I don't think what I said is funny, nor do I think it's necessary he laughs at what I said.

"Oh, Willow..." Jax steps forward. "One, we're not hooking up. In case you forgot, I stopped it from happening tonight, and two, we are going to be friends. I know exactly what you're doing, and unlike your piece of shit ex, I'm not going to allow it to happen."

When I give him a *what the hell are you talking about* look, he says, "Your mom and dad died from cancer. Then you got cancer. Now you don't want marriage or kids. You don't want friends. You would rather be homeless than lean on other people..." He steps towards me. Out of instinct, I step back, but the kitchen is small and my back hits the edge of the counter.

Jax presses his body against mine and pushes a wet strand of hair behind my ear. "You're pushing everyone away, Willow. If you make no connections, nobody can mourn your loss if you die."

I swallow the boulder-sized lump in my throat because he's right and we both know it. Breast cancer wasn't the first cancer my mom was diagnosed with. It was just the one that killed her. Then there's my aunt who died from ovarian cancer, and my uncle who died from brain cancer...

"I'm not letting you push me away," Jax says, his voice filled with conviction. "You're going to live here as long as you need to, and I'm going to be your friend. When you need someone to lean on, I'll be here. Got it?"

My head is telling me to run. Run far and run fast. But my heart, the organ that's craving a connection I've denied myself for too long, is begging me to stay, and like the fool I am, I go with my heart. "Got it."

We head back upstairs, but before I can enter my own room, Jax's hand lands on my shoulder. "You've been alone long enough, Willow. Why don't you come sleep in my bed with me?"

Wordlessly, I allow him to take my hand in his and guide me down the hall to his room. We both climb into his bed and shuffle under the covers. At first, it's awkward, especially since not even a few hours ago we were very close to fucking. But then Jax lifts his arms and scoops up my body, dragging me closer to him. My arm drapes across his torso and my face snuggles into the curve of his shoulder. His fingers run up and down my spine and my eyelids begin to flutter closed. For the first time in too long, I not only feel connected to someone, but I feel safe.

Chapter Five

JAX

WHAT KIND OF FUCKING MAN KICKS A WOMAN out when she's already at her lowest point? When she's just found out she has cancer and is scared for her life? A selfish piece of shit, that's who. I never met Willow's ex, but if I ever find out who he is and see him somewhere, you better fucking believe I'll beat the shit out of him.

I hate that Willow went through having cancer, having surgery, and then all of the treatments alone. Looking back at the past year, it all makes sense now. So many times, I would find her at the shop early in the morning. She was given a key for early appointments, and I would bet she's used the bathroom to rinse off and brush her teeth. After she came back from her vacation, she didn't look well rested at all. Not like you should look when you've just spent weeks relaxing and enjoying your time off. She looked tired, but I didn't even think to ask questions. She's always kept to herself. Sure, we all get along. She's one of us. But looking back, she's always kept everyone at a safe distance. Close enough for us all to know she's a good person, but far enough away that we never really got to know the parts she chose to keep hidden.

Tonight, at the club, she laughed and joked with everyone. They all knew her name, and it was clear she got along with everyone, but she never actually conversed with anyone. She uses them to have a good time. To have a connection without actually connecting. She's so scared of dying, she won't let anyone in.

"When I told him that kids were no longer in my plan, and neither was marriage, he dumped me."

Any smart person can see that Willow was pushing him away in hopes that he would pull her closer. She needed someone strong to hold her tight when she felt like she was drifting away, but instead he cut the rope and let her go. Because he's weak and doesn't deserve her.

My alarm buzzes letting me know it's time to get up. I have an appointment coming in first thing this morning. Willow's side of the bed is empty, so she must have gotten up earlier.

After showering and getting dressed, I head downstairs. The aroma of coffee wafts in the air, and when

I reach the kitchen, I find Willow standing in front of the machine with two cups of coffee in her hands.

"Morning," she says, handing me one of the cups. "Black, just like you like it."

"Thank you." I take a much-needed sip.

While we drink our coffees in silence, I take a moment to check out Willow. She looks the same as she did yesterday before she changed into her club clothes. She's wearing a black Forbidden Ink T-shirt, ripped jeans, and a pair of Converse. On the outside, she looks like she's always looked.

But after everything she's told me, it feels like I'm seeing her in a new light. She's no longer the sweet, delicate woman I always assumed her to be. She's strong and determined and kind of badass. She hides her insecurities and only allows the world to see what she wants them to see.

And instead of allowing herself to wallow in what she's been through, she chooses to live life for today. She laughs and smiles and never lets anything bring her down. She may be ten years younger than me, but with her parents' deaths and having to face cancer on her own, she's far more mature than other women her age.

And then it hits me. I told Willow I wanted to be her friend, but the truth is I want to be more than that. I want to be the man she turns to, leans on, depends on. I want to be the one she lives her todays with. But more than that, I want to be the man who shows her how to find her tomorrow.

"Your face looks like you're thinking so hard you're going to explode," Willow jokes.

"I was." I laugh. "What do you say after work tonight we grab dinner and a movie?"

"You were thinking that hard about asking me out on a date?" She raises a single brow in question.

I want to tell her everything that was really going through my head, but I can already tell Willow is the type of woman to spook easily. I told her I would be her friend, and I'm going to be just that, and over time, once she knows I'm not going anywhere, I'll show her that I not only want her today, but her tomorrow as well.

"Not a date," I correct her, so she won't have an excuse to say no. "Just two friends going to get something to eat and see a movie together."

She rolls her eyes, but when a hint of a smile splays across her face, I know she's going to say yes. "Okay."

THE DAY CRAWLS BY AND I KNOW IT'S BECAUSE I'm looking forward to taking Willow out tonight. Lunch finally rolls around and Evan orders subs from the deli next door. Since Willow and I don't have clients at the moment, she eats with me in the office.

"What movie do you want to see?" I ask her, pulling up the listings on my phone.

"What is there?"

"Romantic comedy, action, horror..." I flip through the different movies. "*The Breakfast Club* is playing too."

"What's that?"

My finger stills and I glance up at her. "You don't know what *The Breakfast Club* is?" And then I remember she's ten years younger than me. "*Pretty In Pink*?" She shakes her head. "*Grease*?" Another shake of her head. "*Stand By Me*?" She shakes her head. "*Sixteen Candles*... every girl has seen that damn movie."

"Nope, haven't seen any of those."

"All right, that's it." I click on the movie and place an order for two tickets. "Your movie education begins tonight with *The Breakfast Club*."

Her smile is wide when she says, "I can't wait."

Jase leaves around three, and then Gage leaves shortly after. Evan stays until around five, when I tell him I'll handle the phones since I don't have any more appointments today. Willow finally comes out of her workstation a little after six. The guy she tattooed is grinning ear-to-ear and talking her ear off about what he plans to get next.

"Everything good?" I ask him as he pulls his credit card out of his pocket to pay.

"Yeah." His eyes stay trained on Willow. "That woman is seriously talented."

"That she is," I agree, pulling up his appointment in the computer, so I can find how much he owes.

Willow points to his name, and when I look up, I notice she's leaning over my shoulder. Her shirt is a V-neck, and her ample cleavage is peaking out of the top. My eyes flit over to her client, who is zeroed in on her tits as well.

"Willow, why don't you go clean up your station while I check this guy out? That way we can leave to go to dinner. We don't want to be late for the movie."

She stands up straight, and in my peripheral vision, I see she's looking at me like I'm crazy, and maybe I am, but I'm not about to sit here and watch this fucker eye-fuck her.

"Thank you for your business," she tells the guy. "Here's my card for when you're ready to schedule your next appointment."

"Does it have your personal number on it?" the guy asks.

His card gets approved, and I hand him his receipt so he can sign it. "No, it's the business number because we're professionals here and don't date clients," I say as I drop a pen onto the receipt for him to use.

The guy signs his name, leaving Willow a decent tip, and takes his card. "Well, if you change your mind—"

I don't let him finish whatever he's about to say. "She won't."

The guy looks over at Willow, probably hoping she'll correct me, but when she doesn't, he just nods and then exits the shop.

"What the hell was that for?" Willow hisses, getting in my face once the door is closed and locked. "I'm pretty sure I have a voice, which means I can speak for myself." She pokes the front of my chest with her pink-painted fingertip that matches the streaks in her hair.

I scoff. "That guy was practically stripping you naked with his eyes."

"And he also tipped me forty percent," she volleys.

"Your work speaks for itself. There's no reason to flirt to get more money. This is a tattoo shop, not a strip club." I eye her shirt, and she glances down. When she looks back up, heat is practically steaming from her ears. Her eyes glaring daggers my way. "It's no different than when you guys let women flirt with you. It keeps them happy and gets you a good tip." She's not wrong, but I'm not about to tell her that. I'm too jealous thinking of all the men who probably ask Willow out. She's young, tatted up, pierced, and beautiful.

Without thinking about what I'm doing, I grip the back of her head and pull her face towards mine, claiming her lips. The kiss starts out soft and slow, but quickly progresses. Teeth clash, tongues duel. Willow's fingers quickly find the button to my jeans at the same time I'm yanking hers down her thighs. This is not how this was supposed to go. I was supposed to befriend her, show her I'm here for her.

Her tiny fingers wrap around my hard dick, and I groan into her mouth. Why is it all this woman has to do

33

is touch me and all rational thought flies out the damn window?

Using my dick like it's a rope she can pull on, she guides us backwards until the back of her legs hit the couch. Needing to taste other parts of her, I wrap her hair in my fingers and tilt her head to the side. As I trail open-mouthed kisses down her slim neck, she strokes my dick. I focus on how sweet she tastes so I don't come in her hand. My nose sniffs her scent. It's sweet. The same perfume she always wears. I already know I'm fucking addicted.

My mouth descends to her collarbone, and I push her shirt and bra strap to the side so I can bite down on her shoulder. She moans in pleasure, so I bite harder.

Not liking her shirt in my way, I yank it up and over her head, then take a second to check out her perfect fucking tits. Scooping one out of her bra cup, I lift it to my mouth and wrap my lips around the pointed, pink nipple. Then I bite down on it. Hard. Willow groans, and her hand squeezes my shaft. *My girl likes it rough...*

"Do it again," she breathes.

Pulling her other tit out of its cup, I take both in my hands and squeeze them together. I can feel Willow's eyes on me. She's watching. Opening my mouth wide, I take both nipples into my mouth and suck on them. Willow squirms, wanting more. I'd bet my left nut, if I dipped my finger into her pussy, she would be dripping wet.

I suck on her nipples again, but this time I scrape my teeth across the hard buds.

"Jesus, Jax."

"I love your fucking tits," I growl just before I suck on them again.

"My turn," she murmurs. Before I can ask her what she means, she drops down onto the sofa, so her face is parallel with my dick. She takes my entire length into her mouth until the tip of my dick hits the back of her throat.

"Willow, fuck. Wait..." I try to get her mouth off me. I'm going to shoot my load right down her pretty little throat. It's been too long since my dick's seen any action aside from my own hand.

She shakes her head and mumbles something with my dick still shoved down her throat, and the vibration sends me over the fucking edge. I watch as Willow swallows down every drop of my cum, then licks the head clean. With hooded eyes, she glances up at me shyly, and if I hadn't just come, I would be now.

Hating that she made me come before I pleasured her, I lift her and throw her onto the couch. Her back hits the leather, and she laughs at my caveman behavior.

"I'm supposed to be a gentleman," I growl, ripping each of her shoes off and then tugging her pants and underwear down her legs and onto the floor. When I drop my body on top of hers, she giggles, something I've never heard from her before. The sound does shit to me, hitting me in places I've never felt.

Taking her bottom lip between my lips, I suck it into my mouth then bite down on it. "A real gentleman always makes sure the woman is taken care of before he is." I kiss my way down her neck, over her breasts—only stopping long enough to give each nipple a lick—and down her belly. I stop when I spot a horizontal scar several inches below her belly button.

She tenses up. "That's from my hysterectomy," she admits.

I give it a kiss. "A beautiful battle wound," I murmur before I continue my descent. When I get to the hood of her neatly trimmed pussy, I give it a soft kiss. When I spread her thighs, I notice two things: one, she's just as I thought—wet as fuck. And two, her clit is pierced.

"Who did this?" I pinch the tight bud between my fingers. The thought of Gage or Evan seeing her sweet pussy has me seeing red.

"I had it done before I started working here."

Dipping my head between her legs, I suck the silver piercing into my mouth. Her back arches and she begs me to make her come.

Not wanting to make her wait any longer, I push two fingers into her pussy at the same time I flick her clit with my tongue. My fingers and mouth work in tangent—licking, fucking, sucking until Willow's body is trembling and she's screaming out my name.

Her hands find my hair and she tugs me against her pussy, grinding herself on my face until her orgasm has passed. When she lets go, I look up at her. Our eyes meet, and I swear my heart actually skips a fucking beat. Her lips are swollen from our kissing and her sucking my dick. Her nipples are red from me biting them. Her eyes are hooded over. Her hair is ruffled like she's just been fucked even though she hasn't been. She looks gorgeous, and my only thought is I need to make this woman mine.

Crawling up her body, I take her face between my hands, careful not to press my weight on top of her. As if she knows exactly what I'm thinking—or maybe she's just thinking the same thing I am—she reaches down and grabs my dick, guiding me into her.

Her pussy is wet and warm, and even though I just finished fingering her, my dick still stretches her out good. Our mouths fuse, and our tongues unite. With my arms on either side of her head, and my hands still cradling her face, I kiss and fuck Willow slowly, deeply. And unlike the frenzied way we both came a few minutes ago, this time we take our time. I make sure I don't come until Willow does, and only once she's moaning and her insides are clenching around my dick, do I let myself follow behind.

When we both come down from our orgasms, and our breathing has calmed, I pull out of Willow and roll to the side so we're both lying on the couch. It's not big, but that's okay because I like her body snuggled up against mine.

After a few minutes, Willow breaks the silence. "I think this was a mistake, Jax."

I take her face and tilt it up to look at me. "No, it

wasn't."

"We were supposed to be friends," she says. If I thought she really meant that, I would backtrack and apologize, but I know why she's saying this—to push me away. She felt what I felt. The connection. I watched it happen with my brother and Celeste when they were younger, and then later when they found each other again, but I never thought it would happen to me. I had accepted some people just aren't meant to fall in love. I have my family, my friends, my tattoo shop. I thought I was okay being unattached. Until now. Until Willow.

It's only been twenty-four hours since she stepped out of the bathroom in the shop and opened my eyes, but I already know she's the one.

"Jax," she prompts when I don't say anything—too lost in my own thoughts. "This thing—"

Not wanting to hear every reason she's about to spew in an attempt to push me away, I cover her mouth with mine. We kiss for a brief moment before I pull back.

When she opens her mouth, I cover it with my hand. "No, I have something I need to say and you're going to listen." Needing to look her in the eyes, I sit us up and pull her naked body onto my lap.

"This is probably the craziest thing I've ever said to anyone," I admit. "And I don't know what's come over me, but I know the words I'm about to speak are one hundred percent true, and I need you to know that." She nods once, but thankfully keeps quiet.

"Willow, you've been through so much, and you went through it all on your own. Your parents having cancer. Then you having to make the scary decision to have a hysterectomy when you found out you also had cancer. I don't blame you for pushing people away. I get it. You're scared. What if you get cancer again? What if someone else you love gets cancer?

"The thing about life is that nothing is a sure thing. We could walk out on to the sidewalk and get hit by a car. But that doesn't mean we live our life alone. You toasted last night to today, but are you even living for today if you don't let anyone in?"

Willow's face softens. She swallows thickly, but doesn't say anything, so I continue. "You don't have to be alone... *We* don't have to be alone. I'm almost forty years old. I've dated dozens of women, but I never saw a future with a single one of them. It wasn't until you stepped out of that bathroom that I realized it was because I was waiting for the right woman. You. I want to be the guy who you live today with. But more than that, I want to be the man who helps you find your tomorrow."

Willow gasps and a tear trickles down her cheek. "I don't know if I can give you that," she admits softly. "I'm so scared."

Framing her face in my hands, I give her a soft kiss to her lips. "How about you just give me today? We'll take it one day at a time, but instead of doing it alone, we'll do it together."

"Okay," she whispers. "Today. Together."

Chapter Six
WILLOW

My head is spinning with everything that's happened. Everything Jax has said. I don't know where up is at this point, but I think I'm okay with that. He wants to live in today with me, and if I'm honest, I really want to live in it with him. I was never one to believe in love at first sight, and I'm not saying I'm in love with him, plus, I've known him for two years... But there's something there between us, and I would be stupid to allow my fear of the future to stop us from seeing where things go. But first, he needs to know a couple of things.

"No marriage," I blurt out. When his brows furrow, I explain. "Marriage means forever. I can live in today with you, but marriage is off the table. So, if that's something you want, you need to know it's never going to happen."

Jax nods once. "I understand. No marriage."

"And I don't want any kids."

"There are other ways of having kids," he says softly.

"If you want kids, you need to walk away now," I tell him. "I don't want kids. Kids are attachments, dependents, and if something happens to one of us, they will be left without a mom or a dad. No kids. Ever." I choke out the last word.

Jax's gaze flits back and forth between my eyes, then he nods. "No kids. Just you and me. Today."

My chest tightens, squeezing my heart. "If you change your mind, it's okay," I tell him, needing him to know he always has an out. "I'll never change my mind, but if you do... if you want marriage and kids, all you have to do is tell me and I'll understand."

"Okay," he says, wrapping his arms around me. "If anything ever changes, I'll tell you." He presses his lips to mine. "We already missed the movie, but how about we get cleaned up, go grab some takeout, and we can go home and rent a movie."

"That sounds good."

When we get home, we both run upstairs to change out of our work clothes. When I go to enter my room, Jax stops me. "I want you in my room with me."

"Do you think we're moving too fast?" I ask, worried we're going to lose control and crash and burn.

"We're living in today," he says. "Today, I want you in

my bed with me."

After moving my duffel bag of stuff into his room, we change and then go back downstairs to eat our Chinese and watch a movie. He doesn't find any of the movies he mentioned before, but he seems stoked when he apparently finds another movie he swears everyone needs to watch before they die: *Top Gun*.

While we watch the movie, Jax holds me close to him. We laugh at the funny stuff the guys do and say. Jax recites his favorite lines along with the guys when they say them, and then when Maverick and Charlie make love, he picks me up, and forgetting about the rest of the movie, carries me up to his room and makes love to me until we're both unable to move. And then once we're both completely sated, we fall asleep wrapped in each other's arms.

Today, I think to myself, *was a really good day.* And then for the first time in over a year, I allow myself to think about tomorrow.

Chapter Seven

JAX

THE FEEL OF SOMETHING RUBBING AGAINST my dick has me waking up. I glance down and grin at the sight of Willow's perfect round ass currently rubbing up and down my dick. I take a moment to appreciate the sight in front of me. She's in a tiny black tank top and an even tinier black thong that leaves her plump butt cheeks completely exposed. She wears the same thing to bed every night—only the colors changing. And every morning she wakes me up in the same way. With her ass against my dick.

It's been a week since she's moved in here. A week of going to bed and waking up together. A week of flirting and fucking. A week of watching classic movies and getting to know each other. She asked that we keep what's happening between us quiet until we know for sure it's going somewhere. Today is a family barbecue, though, and there's no way I'm keeping what's happening between us quiet. It's been hard enough trying to keep my hands off her at work every damn day.

Pushing my boxers down, I release my dick so she's now rubbing skin to skin. My hand grips the curve of her hip, and she stills, knowing I'm now awake. Then she picks up her ministrations again. Rubbing along my length, which is hardening by the second.

My hand glides up her side and over her tit. I squeeze it hard, and she arches her back. I push the top of her tank down and pinch her nipple. Willow tries to remain quiet, but I catch the tiny sigh that escapes her lips, and it makes me smile.

I love her sighs and moans. Anything that tells me I'm making her happy or satisfied. Pleasuring her. Making her feel good. Until Willow, I never much cared about how a woman felt. They were all just warm bodies to sink into. And I never allowed them to spend the night. With my little sister living with me, and then my niece, I never wanted to set a bad example. And if I spent the night at their place, I'd usually leave before they woke up. But with Willow, all I want to do is spend my days and nights in bed with her.

I push Willow's hair out of the way, and then her

thong, and then leaning forward, I spread her thighs enough that I can sink my dick into her from behind. She helps me by propping her foot up onto the side of my thigh. My lips trail kisses along her delicate neck and collarbone as I slowly move in and out of her.

Her soft sighs turn into loud moans. Her ass pushes back against my pelvis, and she meets me thrust for thrust. I grab ahold of her tit again, pinching and pulling on it, before I go lower, dipping my hand beneath the front of her underwear. She's soaking wet. I press my thumb against her swollen clit and massage circles. It only takes a few seconds before she explodes. Her pussy clamps down on my dick and her juices soak my fingers. Knowing she's come, I let myself come as well, shooting my hot seed deep into her.

For a brief moment, an overwhelming sense of sadness hits me, knowing that no matter what we do, no matter how many times I take Willow raw, she'll never be able to get pregnant. Not because I need a child of my own, but because I've seen the way she is around other people's kids, and I know she would make a damn good mom. And because of something out of her control, whether it's genetic or science or whatever, she's been robbed of that chance.

And I vow in this moment to make sure every today with Willow is filled with so much love and happiness, she'll never for a second miss what she can't have.

"So, you and Willow, huh?" Jase asks, leaning up against the wall of his back patio. I was going to announce our being together at the barbecue, but then I got worried of how they might react. So, instead, I texted him and Quinn to let them know, so when we showed up, they wouldn't be shocked and make Willow feel uncomfortable. I should've known, though, they would have my back. We always have each other's back.

"I didn't see it coming," I admit, watching her, Celeste, and Skyla wading in the pool, probably gossiping about God knows what. "But she's fucking amazing."

"And young," he adds, his tone clear of judgment.

"Ten years younger, but she's been through a lot. She's probably more mature than the both of us combined," I joke. I'm glad when he doesn't ask me to explain because it's not my story to tell, and I won't tell Willow's story unless she tells me it's okay.

"If you're happy then I'm happy." He pats me on the shoulder. "I have to ask, though. What happens if it doesn't work out? How will that work with her being employed by us?"

"It will work out," I tell him. "She's the one, man. No doubt about it."

Jase's cell phone goes off and he pulls it out of his pocket to check it. "Quinn can't make it. Rick needs her at some function." He rolls his eyes.

"Leave her alone. She's in love, and they're still newlyweds."

"She can be in love, and they can be newlyweds... Doesn't mean she has to completely cut us out of her life."

"Dad, come in the pool!" Skyla yells.

"Duty calls," Jase says, shrugging his shirt off and running towards the pool. With his legs tucked under him, he jumps into the water, splashing all of the women. Celeste shrieks, Skyla laughs, and Willow splashes him back.

Willow's eyes meet mine and I nod toward the door. Her eyes light up, but she shakes her head, knowing exactly what I want. I nod and her grin gets wider. I make sure she's going to follow me in and then I head inside to wait for her.

When I hear her bare feet slapping against the marble floor, I reach out and grab her arm, pulling her into the bathroom and slamming the door behind us.

"Jax, we can't do this here!" She giggles.

"We can and we are." I lift her onto the edge of the sink, and waste no time pulling her wet bathing suit bottoms down her legs and pushing the tiny triangles covering her pert tits to the side, exposing her taut pink nipples. As I lean down, taking a nipple into my mouth, Willow's nails scrape along the scalp of my newly shaved head. I suck on her nipple then give the other one attention.

"Jax, you have to hurry up," Willow whines breathlessly. She's afraid of getting caught. While I don't really give a shit, I don't want her to feel uncomfortable.

I push my swim trunks down enough my dick pops out, hard and ready to be inside Willow's perfect pussy. She spreads her legs open for me, and I pull her to the edge of the counter. She grips my shaft and guides me into her. The feeling of her tight pussy wrapped around my dick is absolute fucking perfection. I could live inside this woman.

Once I'm completely seated in her, she wraps her arms around my neck and kisses me. Knowing we don't have much time, my thumb goes straight to her pierced clit. As I fuck her slow and deep, I massage circles along her swollen nub, once in a while tugging on the metal jewel. She's soaking wet, and I can feel her juices dripping down my balls.

"Oh my—" She begins to scream out her climax, and normally I love the way she lets go, but I know she'll regret it once she's come down from her orgasmic high. So, I fuse our mouths together, muffling her screams, as we both find our release.

Chapter Eight
WILLOW

I ALWAYS THOUGHT JAX WAS A BORING OLD man. Sexy, but boring. But I was wrong. He's anything but boring. And he's an animal in bed. He loves to fuck me everywhere. All over the house, in his office at the shop, the bathroom in his brother and sister-in-law's house, and right now, in the movie theater.

"Baby," he whispers into my ear, "just pull that skirt up and sit on my dick."

I stifle a laugh, not wanting to draw attention to us. The theater is almost empty since we're seeing an older movie that's on its way out. There's only one younger couple in the middle and one more all the way in the front. Jax and I are sitting in the back corner. It's dark, and nobody would probably notice...

"C'mon," he purrs, running his hand up my thigh and under my skirt. He pushes the thin material of my panties to the side and inserts a couple of fingers inside me.

When I moan softly, he shakes his head and pulls his fingers out of me. I pout, wanting him back inside me. With those same fingers, he brings them up to my lips. "Shh... You have to be quiet." He rubs the pads of his fingers along my lips, wetting them with my juices, and I squirm in my seat.

"Come here, Willow," he whispers, and this time I do as he says. He lifts my skirt up slightly and pushes my panties to the side, and when I sit in his lap, his dick impales me.

He must know I'm going to moan or scream because he covers my mouth with his hand. It's the hand that was just inside me and I can smell myself on his fingers. "You have to be quiet," he warns, just before he moves his hand and pushes into me from the bottom. I hold onto the armrests as Jax slowly thrusts in and out of me. My eyes flit between the two couples who are oblivious to what's happening behind them and the front door, afraid an employee will walk in.

Jax reaches around and finds my clit. Using my juices to help create friction, he rubs my clit until I'm coming all over his fingers and dick. A couple more thrusts and I can feel his warmth shooting inside of me.

He lifts me from his lap, and I feel the cum trickling

down the inside of my thigh. Grabbing a napkin, I wipe it up the best I can, then excuse myself to the bathroom to clean up better.

When I get back, Jax is watching the movie with a big grin splayed across his face. I sit back down, and he feeds me a piece of buttery popcorn. "What's happening in the movie?" I ask, trying to play catch up.

"I have no clue." Jax shrugs. "I guess we'll have to see it again."

Chapter Nine
WILLOW

PINK BALLOONS. PINK STREAMERS. PINK CAKE. Pink cupcakes. Pink is everywhere. Which makes sense, since Celeste and Jase found out they're having twin girls. I've just never seen so much freaking pink in one place before.

I watch Celeste laugh at something one of her friends is saying. She throws her head back, so carefree and happy. She looks adorable, dressed in her designer pink and black dress, with her baby bump popping out. Jase is standing next to her, with his arms around her—one of his hands rubbing the bump. I swallow a bitter tasting lump in my throat. I'm happy for them, but it's still a hard reality to swallow that I'll never be pregnant. I'll never have my own baby to love. I've accepted my decision to never have kids, but it doesn't mean I don't occasionally feel sad or envious of others.

"I got you a cupcake," Jax says, sitting next to me on the couch. I jump slightly, lost in my own world, and he gives me a curious look. "You okay?" he asks, his tone laced with worry. Not pity, though, which is one of the reasons I love being with Jax. It's been four months since we've been together and not once has he ever looked at me with pity over my situation.

"Yeah," I tell him, taking the pink cupcake from him and giving him a fake smile.

He can see right through me though, and he frowns. One thing I've learned about Jax is he doesn't like to see me upset, ever. When I don't give him anything more, choosing to focus on my cupcake instead, he doesn't say a word.

We spend the next hour talking to everyone we know. Quinn and her husband, Rick, show up late, and when he tells her they need to get going, Jax and I decide to leave as well. We say our goodbyes to the happy couple and then walk outside with Quinn and Rick.

"How's the photography business going?" I ask Quinn as we walk down the sidewalk to their vehicle. She started a photography company a few years back and has been working hard at building it up.

Quinn glances back at Rick then says, "I've actually decided to put that on hold."

"What? Why?" Jax asks.

"Well, with Rick and I trying to have a baby, we felt it would be best if I stay home."

"*We* felt or he felt?" Jax accuses, glaring daggers at Rick, whose jaw tightens in anger. "You know you can have a family and work." He points towards the house. "Look at Celeste and Jase. They're doing it."

"What my wife and I decide is between us," Rick says, taking Quinn's hand in his. "We need to go."

Quinn opens her mouth to argue but then closes it. "Bye," she says softly.

"She's changed," I tell Jax, remembering how lively Quinn used to be. In the past, we'd been out a couple times together and she was the life of the party. Laughing and drinking and having a good time. Now, it's as if she's a scared turtle hiding inside her shell.

"Yeah," he agrees. "I just don't know what to do about it."

Taking my hand in his, we walk down the street to the subway station to go home. Jax is quiet the entire ride home, and once we're inside, he remains quiet.

"What's going on?" I ask him, climbing onto his lap and straddling his thighs.

His eyes meet mine and he frowns, almost as if he's warring with himself as to whether he should tell me what's on his mind.

"Talk to me," I insist. Jax has quickly become my go-to person and I would like to think he feels the same way. He's not just the guy I'm sleeping with. He's my best friend. The person I wake up with every morning and go to bed with at night. He's become a part of me.

"You could have what Celeste and Jase have," he says softly. It takes a couple times of repeating his words in my head to properly string them together. And when I do, I try to back up. But Jax wraps his arms around me and holds me close to him.

"Just hear me out," he says, but I'm already shaking my head. "Please," he begs.

"Jax…" I begin, but I'm stunned into silence when he reaches into his pocket and pulls out a diamond ring.

"I love you, Willow," he says, his eyes locked with mine. "We could get married and adopt a couple of kids. I make enough money. We could have a house full of kids if that's what you wanted."

A golf ball-sized lump blocks my airpipe. I can't talk or swallow or even breathe. I told him what I wanted, and he said okay. So, why is he doing this now?

I scamper off his lap and stand, crossing my arms over my chest and willing myself not to cry. "I told you I didn't want to get married or have kids. You know this. Why are you doing this? You're ruining everything."

Jax leans forward, and gripping me by my hips, pulls me back into his lap. "Willow, I know what you said, but I saw the look in your eyes today. You can't tell me deep down you don't want that. The marriage, the kids, the family."

"Is that what you want?" I ask.

"I want whatever you want." He takes my face in his hands and kisses me softly before he pulls back. "This ring isn't a proposal."

When I give him a confused look, he continues, "I'm okay with what we have. I'm more than okay with it. I love you and I love our life together. But I need you to know that if you ever change your mind, if you ever want more, I want to be the one to give that to you."

He takes my hand in his and opens it up, so my palm is facing up. Then, he places the ring in the center. "I bought this ring because I want you to know I love our todays, but I also want your tomorrows. If you never decide to put it on, that's okay. I'll still be here. Always."

He pulls a chain out of the box and loops the ring through the chain. Then he puts it around my neck and links it together. He leans forward and kisses the ring, which is resting against my chest. "I love you, Willow."

Tears burn my eyelids and then fall down my cheeks. Jax uses his thumbs to wipe them up before he kisses me again. The kiss is intense, as if he's trying to convey through his lips and tongue how much he loves me. And I let him. I get lost in our kiss until our lips are numb and our bodies are entangled in one another. We shed our clothes until we're both naked and then Jax makes love to me, whispering how much he loves me and needs me. And it hits me that somewhere along the way I stopped living for today and started looking forward to tomorrow.

And with that thought, I want to run, because looking forward to tomorrow is scary. It means I'm feeling. Letting someone in. It means I'm setting myself and him up for heartbreak when something goes wrong.

As if he can feel me drifting, Jax pushes himself into me deeper, and his lips finds my ear. "You're not going anywhere, Willow. You're going to stay right here with me and live for today."

"Jax," I whimper, finding my release.

He grunts out his own release then stills. "No, baby. If we never get married, that's okay. I just need you to know that whatever you want, I will make sure you have it. Always."

He rolls off me and pulls me into his arms, my back against his chest. His scruffy face nuzzles into my neck, and when his breathing evens out, I know he's asleep.

I consider leaving. Running. And I should. He might not have officially proposed, but it's still a proposal. There's a ring hanging from my neck with the promise of tomorrow.

But instead of running, I snuggle back into Jax and close my eyes, needing him to hold me while I figure out what to do next.

Chapter Ten

JAX
PRESENT DAY

"I REMEMBER WHEN I GAVE YOU THAT RING." I find myself grinning at the memory. "I thought for sure I was going to wake up and you would be gone. But you weren't."

Willow smiles. "I considered it, but I loved you too much to let you go."

"But you didn't say yes," I say, remembering the next morning when we woke up.

Chapter Eleven

JAX

NINE AND A HALF YEARS AGO

"My answer is no," Willow tells me, holding the ring and necklace out to me.

"I didn't ask you to marry me," I say, taking a bite of my cereal. "I told you when you want to, I'll be here. That ring is for you to wear around your neck as a reminder of how much I love you, and one day, if or when you're ready, I hope you'll wear it on your finger."

Willow's brows furrow. "I don't want to have kids, Jax."

"You already told me that." I take another bite of my cereal.

"I know, but I really meant it."

"Okay, then you meant it." I shrug.

"That means no kids for you as long as you're with me."

I know what she's trying to do. Push me away. But it's not going to happen. What Willow doesn't understand is that all I need in my life is her. I'm completely content to spend my days with—and in—her. Kids, no kids. Marriage, no marriage. It doesn't matter. I just needed her to know that whatever she wants, I want that too.

"Willow." I set my spoon down and look at her. "I already know all of this, and I don't care. As long as I have you, I'm good." I push my chair back then pull her onto my lap. "Do you like the ring?"

A tiny smile curls on her lips. "It's beautiful," she breathes. "I just can't do it." Her eyes land in her lap and I lift her chin so she's looking at me.

"That's okay, baby. It's an open invitation."

"An invitation to what?" she asks.

"To share my last name." I shoot her a playful wink.

Chapter Twelve

JAX
PRESENT DAY

"I've spent the last ten years living for today with you," Willow says. "You've given me everything I could ever want or need. A family. Nieces. Sisters. A home." Tears flow down her cheeks like a beautiful waterfall. "But I'm ready for more. I'm ready to share your last name. I'm ready to finally find our tomorrow."

"Oh, Willow." I cup her cheek with my hand. "What do you think we've been doing for the last ten years?" I peck her lips. "We already found it, baby, but it's nice to hear you admit it."

"So, will you marry me?" she asks.

Taking the ring from the table where she set it down, I slide it up her ring finger. Over the years, I've gotten used to seeing it around her neck, but fuck if it doesn't look even more gorgeous on her finger. "Yes, Willow, it would be my honor to marry you."

Willow grins wide. "When?"

"When, what?"

"When can we get married?" Her smile widens.

I laugh at her excitement. "How about tomorrow?"

"Tomorrow?" Her eyes go wide.

"We have nothing holding us back, baby. Let's book a flight to Vegas and say I do."

Willow laughs. "Okay." She nods up and down. "Tomorrow."

Keep reading for a preview of
Jase's and Quinn's stories...

On the Surface

Chapter One

CELESTE

"Two weeks until I'm finally Mrs. Shaw." Olivia squeals loud enough that the patrons sitting at the table next to us look over. Her hands clasp together in excitement as her eyes run along everyone at the table and land on her fiancé, Nicholas Shaw, who is known to most as the newly retired quarterback from the New York Brewers.

To me, though, he's my childhood best friend. Despite our four-year age difference, I've spent the last two decades following Nick around while he's chased his dream of playing pro ball, and I've chased mine of becoming a model. There was even a short span of time when we almost got married—a stupid decision on both our parts, stemmed from a teenage pact in a moment of weakness.

Of course, that was all before he met Olivia, who swooped in with her sweet and adorable self and stole his heart—while simultaneously winning me over and becoming one of the few people I call a friend. She and Nick are expecting their second baby in September. Their son, Reed, is eighteen months old, and at home with his grandparents tonight.

In response to what Olivia says, Nick snakes his arm around her shoulders in a protective manner and pulls her into his side with a wide grin. His lips press against hers softly in a loving gesture, and I'm almost positive they've just given me a cavity from all the sweetness that's radiating off them.

"Which means a bachelorette party is in order!" Olivia's best friend, Giselle, states. She's also pregnant— due in November—and someone I consider a friend.

Her husband, Killian Blake—who is a receiver for the Brewers—also wraps his arm around his wife and pulls her in for a kiss. Only theirs is more intense, more passionate. I can't help but watch as things between them become heated. It's one of those kisses where you want to look away to give them their privacy, but you can't stop watching. *Yep! I've definitely got a cavity, maybe two.*

It isn't until Nick clears his throat that they come up for air. Giselle's face is bright red—not sure if it's out of embarrassment over their public display of affection, or if she's turned on—either way, she's completely captivated by her husband.

"Oh, I don't know." Olivia's nose scrunches up, and she shakes her head. "I'm half-baked." She points to her protruding belly. "And you're pregnant too." She eyes Giselle. "The only person who'll actually get to party is Celeste!" She laughs, shooting me a soft smile.

My gaze goes to my—and I use the term loosely—boyfriend, Chad Vacanti. Chad is forty-five years old and the VP for the investment banking firm he's a partner in. We met at a function we were both attending and hit it off.

Shortly after, I left for the UK to promote my clothing line that went international. Apparently, he had some business over there as well and reached out. We spent several weeks together—when we weren't both working eighteen-hour days—and decided to keep things going when we returned.

It's worked out well for both of us—giving us someone to attend functions with and get lost in after long days of work. He's a lot like me and knows the score, so there aren't any hurt feelings. Chad's nearly twenty years my senior, which is the way I prefer it. Older men tend to have their shit together and are far more mature than the guys my age.

"And it will stay that way," I say with conviction in response to Olivia's comment. Chad looks up from his phone as I finish saying the words, completely focused on work and having no clue what the conversation is about.

"What will stay what way?" he questions—apparently, he's somewhat good at multitasking—good to know he at least hears me when I speak.

"My getting pregnant." His eyes go wide in fear, completely misunderstanding. "That I *won't* be getting pregnant anytime soon," I clarify, and he lets out a harsh sigh of relief, as if having a baby with me would be the absolute worst thing in the world. It's not as if I would want to have kids with him—or with anyone for that matter—but Jesus, does he have to look so relieved?

Taking a bite of my shrimp salad, I try to ignore the four pairs of eyes staring at me—not including Chad's, as his are already back on his phone. It's no secret I'm the odd one out in our group of friends. Unlike Olivia and Giselle, who are both happily doing their part to add to the ever-growing human race, I have no desire to ever procreate.

I have one goal in this life: to make something of myself. Which I happen to think I'm doing a damn good job at. I've learned over the years that independence is the key to a woman's success.

While Chad is decent in bed and someone I can talk business with, he'll never be anything more than that. I don't need him—or any man for that matter. I push back the thoughts of the one guy I allowed myself to need and how that turned out...*with my heart broken and my future nearly destroyed.*

"I still say we need to throw a party!" Giselle insists. "We can do a combined bachelor and bachelorette party at an upscale club." She stops talking, so I look up, and she's giving Olivia the stink-eye. "And not at a strip club."

A loud laugh escapes me as I remember not too long ago when Olivia convinced Nick to take her to Assets, a high-end strip club. I thought he was going to kill me when I surprised her with a lap dance. The poor guy wasn't sure whether to be turned on or upset that his fiancée was thoroughly enjoying another woman grinding on her.

"No, not at a strip club," Olivia agrees. "But it would be fun for all of us to go out and have a good time before we get married." She looks at Nick, who of course nods in agreement. She could tell him she wants him to participate in a shit-eating contest and the guy would nod in agreement if it meant making her happy.

"Mind if I invite Jase?" Killian asks. It doesn't go unnoticed that his gaze quickly meets mine before he looks away. The hairs on the back of my neck stand at the mention of that name. *Jase Crawford.* The one who... I shake myself out of my thoughts, refusing to even finish that sentence. He doesn't deserve a place in my thoughts, in my head, in my... Nope, not going there. He's nothing more than a mistake from my past. A lesson learned the hard way.

"I saw him yesterday at the shop," Killian says, "while getting some work done. Seems like he doesn't get out much."

"Of course he's welcome to come!" Olivia says, speaking for Nick. "He's also invited to the wedding." Her hand comes up and rests on top of Nick's. "After we ran into him on Giselle's birthday, he and Nick have been keeping in touch again. Jax and Quinn are both invited as well."

Jax and Quinn are Jase's brother and sister. They own a tattoo shop here in New York called Forbidden Ink. We went there the night of Giselle's birthday so she and Olivia could get their first tattoo. Olivia chickened out, but Giselle ended up getting a beautiful quote across her upper back just below her nape.

"How many people are coming?" I ask, trying to remain calm, even though the reality of having to see Jase at the wedding has me feeling anything but. "I thought you were keeping it small and intimate."

Nick doesn't speak to his parents, which only leaves Olivia's family and their friends. She didn't want something huge, which could easily happen since Nick's a four-time Super Bowl champion and Olivia's dad is an NFL coach. And then there's her mom—who is no longer alive. She was a huge international supermodel—one I spent many years looking up to. So you can imagine how many people they're acquainted with.

"Only about a hundred and fifty people. We're still keeping it small." She gives me a questioning look. "Jase isn't in the wedding party if that's what you're worried about."

"I'm not," I say far too quickly. Everyone's gazes swing over to me—except Chad, who's still typing away on his phone. "I'm not," I repeat in a tone that makes it clear to drop whatever they're all thinking. It makes sense that Jase and his siblings are invited since Nick has been friends with them since high school.

"I like your new hair color," Olivia says, changing the subject. "It makes you look less...harsh."

"Less like an evil witch?" I wink, and she laughs. When Olivia and I first met, Nick referred to me as the evil witch in their story, and I've yet to live the nickname down. So I figure, if I can't beat them, I might as well join them. But she's right, the black hair gave me an edgier look, which is what the modeling agency I used to be signed with was going for. Since I'm no longer signed with anyone, and I'm free to do as I want with my hair, I dyed it back to my original color—a mahogany brown with hints of auburn mixed in.

"Yes! I mean you can totally pull off any color, obviously, but this color is really pretty."

"Thanks."

"Hey Chad," Giselle calls out from across the table. He looks up to see who said his name. "What do you think about Celeste's hair?"

Chad looks over at me in confusion. "It looks nice," he says with a shrug.

"What does?" she presses.

"Uh...the length?" he says, but it comes out more like a question. "Did you get it cut or something?"

"Actually, it's a different color," Giselle points out— with a big fake smile—before I can answer. It's no secret my friends aren't a fan of Chad's. Olivia is too sweet to say anything mean, but Giselle has no problem calling him out.

"Really?" he asks.

"Yep," I say, taking a bite of my food.

The rest of the meal is spent with everyone hammering out the details for the party, but my mind can't get off the fact that Jase and Nick are hanging out again. He's going to be invited to the party. And he's going to come to the wedding.

I try to think of a reason to get out of going to either one, but I know I can't do that. Nick has been there for me my entire life. I'm not just going to ditch one of the biggest days of his life because of who will be in attendance. I refuse to be affected by this. Jase will just be another guest attending the wedding.

Of course, since I'm in the wedding party as Olivia's bridesmaid, I'm going to have to walk down the aisle in front of everyone, including Jase. I've walked down a million runways at fashion shows—sometimes more than half-naked. I've been on dozens of billboards and in more commercials than I can count. Yet, the thought of having to walk down the aisle, knowing Jase will be there—most likely with a date—has me feeling sick to my stomach. He shouldn't make me feel like this. Not after all this time. Not after the way things ended.

When the bill is paid, everyone makes their way outside to say their goodbyes. Chad's driver comes around and we slide into the back of his town car.

Since it's Saturday night, I'd usually go back to his place, but tonight I tell him I'm going home instead. He simply nods, not even questioning why I'm canceling our evening plans. He doesn't ask if anything is wrong. The entire drive he's on his phone. His arm never snakes around my shoulders like Nick's did to Olivia. His hand never touches mine like Olivia's did to Nick. And when his driver drops me off in front of my building, he doesn't kiss me the way Killian kissed Giselle.

After showering and changing into silky pajamas, I pour myself a glass of white wine to help calm my nerves before bed. Usually, this is when I go through my emails. I confirm my meetings and engagements with Margie, my assistant, for the upcoming week, since she doesn't work Sundays.

I check my company's financials to make sure we're where we need to be. But tonight, I do none of that. Instead, I head outside onto my balcony, which overlooks Central Park. With my condo being on the tenth floor, I'm able to just barely make out the people bustling about. Some are walking their dogs; others are strolling hand-in-hand. It's dark out, just after ten o'clock, but this is the city that never sleeps.

I take in a deep breath, then bring my lips up to my glass, swallowing a taste of the fruity wine. This is what I wanted. A sky-rise condo in Lennox Hills overlooking Central Park. And I finally got it. The day I signed the papers on this condo, I felt like I'd finally made it. I purchased it on my own, with my own credit and my own money.

Yet, as I look out at the luscious trees that fill the park, it feels like every goal and dream I've ever made wasn't enough. I should feel complete, fulfilled. I should feel accomplished. But I don't. I feel empty.

After I finish my wine, I rinse the glass out then climb into bed. I lay here for several minutes, trying to figure out what's wrong with me. I barely even touched my cell phone tonight. *That's because you were too busy watching the sickeningly-sweet couples at the table.* Usually I don't pay attention to how the couples around me act with each other. I don't care whether Chad pays attention to me, or if he kisses me goodbye.

I snuggle into my blankets, trying my hardest not to remember a time when I wanted nothing more than to be one-half to a sickeningly-sweet couple. When my world, for just a brief moment, was filled with hand-holding and kissing and sweet words whispered to one another. I close my eyes, refusing to let the tears come, only my heart—and tear ducts—seem to have a mind of their own, and when the memories of him surface, the tears fall of their own accord.

Chapter Two

CELESTE
THE PAST

"Tell me everything!" I bounce up and down on Nick's bed in his old room in his parents' house. He's home for my graduation, and I'm beyond excited to have my best friend back—even if it's only for a short time. He may only live a hundred miles away, and in the same state, but without me having my own vehicle, it might as well be a million miles away. This past year without Nick has been excruciatingly difficult. I've lost my best friend, the person I talk to and hang out with. He's now an uber-famous professional football player, and I'm just a high school senior.

"You know everything." He laughs. "We talk every day." He strips out of his sweatpants and shirt he wore for his drive over and into a pair of distressed jeans and a collared shirt.

"It's not the same," I whine. "You're living this amazing

life, and I'm stuck here in Piermont without you." I pout. Up until this last year, Nick and I have always lived close enough that I could take the bus, or bum a ride from someone, to visit him. He even went to college locally at North Carolina University. Now, though, things have changed.

"I need details," I beg. "Tell me about the traveling, the money, the fame. I saw you on TMZ at a charity function in New York with Alessandra Starr!" I sigh. Alessandra Starr is an up-and-coming model. She was a lot like me—a nobody from a small town—trying to make a name for herself. She was at the right place at the right time, and boom! Now she's the face of several different companies, including MAC and Lancôme.

"She's not really my type," Nick admits, as if I care about who his type is. I want to know what it's like, not who he's in love with this week.

"Nicholas Shaw!" I shriek. "I don't care who you like or don't like. I want to know about New York… about the event! Did you meet a lot of famous people? When you travel, do you get to order room service? Did you go to any popular clubs? What's it like to see your name and picture plastered all over the magazines?"

Nick rolls his eyes and sits next to me on his bed. "You know I don't care about any of that. I'm doing what I love. Playing ball." It's my turn to roll my eyes. I shouldn't have expected Nick to understand. He was raised with money. To him, this is all just another day in the life of Nicholas

Shaw. He might be my best friend—and our moms might be best friends—and we might've grown up only a few miles apart—on opposite sides of the train tracks—but we might as well be from two different planets.

"I have a surprise for you." He grins wide and stands, then walks over to his luggage. He pulls an envelope from it and hands it to me. Just as my fingers are about to grasp the paper, he pulls it back and laughs.

"Nick!" I growl. "Give it to me."

Chuckling, he hands the envelope to me, this time letting me take it from him.

I open it and read over the document once, twice, a third time. This can't be real. "Nick," I whisper, "what did you do?" Tears form in my eyes. The paper falls from my hands, and my arms wrap around his neck. "Is this for real?"

"It is." He laughs. "I had to do a photoshoot with Elite for Movado, and while I was there, I ended up having brunch with Alessandra and Brenna Myers.

I gasp. "Brenna Myers? As in *the* Brenna Myers...the VP of Elite?" Elite is one of the top modeling agencies in the world.

"Yep. I mentioned I have a friend who would give her left arm to get her foot in the door..."

"Please tell me you didn't make me sound desperate, Nick," I chide.

He laughs some more. "Give me some credit," he says. "Anyway, Elite has a summer internship program, and after showing her your photos, she opened up a spot for you."

"Ohmigod!!!" I squeal. "I can't believe it. This is really happening." I hug Nick again. "Thank you so much!" I grab the paper from the floor, where it fell, and read it again and again. This is actually happening. I'm going to graduate and get out of this hellhole. I'm going to New York!

"Wait," I say, thinking about the details. "Where am I going to live?" This is New York we're talking about. I doubt I can even afford a cardboard box there.

"While you're in the summer program, you'll be living in an apartment with the other girls. It'll all be paid for by Elite. Once it ends, if I need to help you, I will. Don't worry about that now, though," he says, reassuring me. "Just focus on your dreams."

I don't even realize I'm full-on crying until Nick swipes a falling tear with his thumb. "Celeste, I know this is what you want, but trust me when I say, being famous isn't all it's cracked up to be. Everybody is so damn fake." His voice is soft, non-judgmental. He's simply being honest—as honest as he can be as a man who's grown up with money, while I've grown up in a trailer park. "I thought once I was away from my parents it would be different," he adds. "The women are all fake. Alessandra... she's fake." Nick frowns in disappointment.

"I told you once, and I'll tell you again," I say, "the world revolves around money and status, and until you accept that, you're going to keep getting your heart broken and being disappointed." While Nick is looking for love—some non-existent soulmate to give his sappy heart to—I'm looking for a future.

"And I'll tell you once again, we'll have to agree to disagree." He pulls me into a side-hug and kisses my temple. "One day you're going to meet a guy who's going to knock you right off your feet, and you're going to finally understand that no amount of money can buy love."

"That sounds like it would hurt," I joke. "I'll leave the falling to you...on the football field." I shoot him a playful wink, and he laughs. "So, what's going on tonight?" I nod toward his outfit. He's obviously dressed up for a reason. Unless Nick is going somewhere, he's always in basketball shorts and a T-shirt.

"Party tonight. Some friends from high school are getting together for a reunion of sorts." He pulls on his shoes. "Wanna go?"

"Hmm, let's see here..." I tap my lower lip with my index finger, pretending to contemplate whether I want to go. This is the first time I'll get to meet Nick's high school friends. Because of our age difference, he'd never let me tag along to any of the parties he attended while he was in high school or college. "Rich, hot, older guys all in one place, or another night spent with my drunken mother...What do you think?"

Nick frowns. "How is Beatrice?"

"Same as she's been my entire life. Drunk and waiting

on the love of her life to mend her broken heart."

His frown deepens. "You could be a little more understanding."

"Seriously?" I scoff. "Some biker guy knocks up my mother and takes off, promising to return, only to disappear. My mom chooses to pine after him for the next eighteen years, forcing me to live in a rusted metal can in a damn trailer park, barely working enough to pay our electric bill and rent, and I'm supposed to be understanding?"

My blood is now boiling, and my skin is heating up. My mother could've gotten us out of our shitty situation. She's best friends with Victoria, Nick's mom. She's been introduced to dozens of wealthy men.

But instead, she refuses to leave our seven hundred square foot trailer, and continues to work at the same hole-in-the-wall diner, in hope that one day he'll come back like he promised.

I've tried to look him up a couple times at the public library, but the only thing I know is that his last name is Leblanc—same as mine. Apparently, he once referred to me as baby Leblanc, and when my mom asked, he confirmed that was his last name.

According to my mom, he was a member of some biker gang and went by the name of Snake—*really classy, huh?* He met my mom while passing through town. They fell in love and spent the next few months planning their life together. My mom got pregnant, and supposedly Snake was just as excited as she was. He said he had some affairs to get in order, promising to return soon, only he never did—making my mother a single mom. And yes, in case you're wondering, Snake is actually written on my birth certificate. Who in their right mind falls in love with a man but never takes the time to learn his real name? My mother, that's who!

"I get it," Nick says, "but you've never been in love, so you don't understand."

"And you have?" I snort in disbelief.

"No, but I'm at least capable of it," Nick volleys back. "If I met the love of my life and she promised to return, I would wait for her. Your mom is heartbroken. She can't imagine loving anyone else but him. It's kind of romantic."

"Yeah, well, if that's how love works, you can have it," I hiss. "Her love for my *father* destroyed her, and I refuse to ever be destroyed by a man."

"No, you'd rather *do* the destroying," Nick smarts.

"What's that supposed to mean?" I snap. It's not often Nick and I argue, but when we do, it's usually over this very subject. We don't see eye-to-eye on love and never will.

"Never mind." Nick sighs. "Just try not to *destroy* any of my friends' hearts tonight. I prefer to keep them as friends."

"I can't help if they fall for me and get hurt." I turn on my heel, done with this conversation. "I need to run home and change my outfit. Drive me?"

"Sure."

We pull up to my place, and Nick parks his Audi along the road since my mom's piece of shit clunker is parked in the tiny driveway. She's sitting outside with a beer in one hand and a joint in the other, and our neighbor Dale—the nasty drug dealer I know she fucks on occasion when she's feeling extra lonely—is sitting next to her with his hand resting on her thigh.

"Want me to go in with you?" Nick offers.

Anyone else and I wouldn't have even let him bring me here, but Nick has seen my home more times than I can count, so it's pointless to hide it from him. I'm not sure why our moms have remained friends over the years, but it's the one thing I'm grateful for. Their friendship was the only good part of my life growing up. Nick's mom has always treated me like I'm her own daughter—always including me in their trips and holidays.

"No." I shake my head. "I'll be quick. Plus, we might come out and find your car to be missing." I laugh humorlessly, and Nick rolls his eyes.

I jump out of the passenger seat and head up the sidewalk. My mom notices me and gives me a small smile. "Hey, pretty girl," she coos.

I bend at the waist and give her a kiss on her forehead. I want to hate her for this life—and many days it feels like I do—but then she smiles and calls me *pretty girl* and my heart breaks for her. She fell in love and got her heart broken. If you want to know what a broken heart is capable of, spend a day with my mom. It looks just like this: a once beautiful, vibrant woman who was full of life, burnt into ash. With wrinkles around her lips from smoking, and dark circles under her eyes from never feeling rested or content, she's nothing more than the rubble left after the fire—which has ruined everything it's come in contact with—has finally gone out.

I've never personally experienced the former version of my mother, but I've heard about the woman she used to be. And oftentimes, when I was younger, I'd wish that one day I would get to experience that woman for myself. But now that I'm older, I know that once something's been burnt to ash, there is no coming back.

"What are you and Nick up to?" she asks, taking a hit of her joint and then passing it to Dale.

"Going to a party."

"That was nice of him to come in for your graduation. Victoria said she's going to host a gathering at her place for you afterward."

"Sounds good," I say, giving her a fake smile. "I'm going to go change."

Stepping into the trailer, beads of sweat instantly surface on my skin. I check the thermostat and it shows eighty-nine degrees. I try the light switch to see if the AC is broken or if the electric is out. The light doesn't come on. *Damn it, Mom!* She didn't pay the electric bill.

I try the water and no such luck. She didn't pay that either. Looks like I'm going to have to dip into my savings to pay it. I have no clue what she's going to do once I leave for New York, but my hope is that once I hit it big, I'll be able to convince her to move with me, or at the very least, buy her a better place to live in. Although, if I'm honest, I know she won't allow either option to happen. That would mean moving out of this piece-of-shit place, and if she hasn't moved yet, I doubt she ever will.

After changing into a cute yet sexy burgundy tank dress that Nick's mom bought me for my eighteenth birthday last month, and sliding on a pair of cute wedges, I use a bottle of water to quickly brush my teeth, then head out.

When I step outside, the cool air sends goosebumps running up my arms. I give my mom a knowing look as I dab my forehead with a paper towel.

"Sorry," she whispers, her face filled with apology. She's said the word so many times over the years, it's been desensitized.

Once I'm back in Nick's car, he takes off to his friend Jared's house, which is in the same gated community Nick's parents live in. Apparently, Jared's parents are on a cruise and he has the house to himself. Most of Nick's friends are still in college. The only reason he's not is because he was drafted into the NFL at the end of his junior year and currently plays for Carolina. When we pull up, the street is already packed with expensive cars that line both sides of the road.

"How long do you give it until someone calls the

cops?" I joke.

"Maybe another hour." Nick laughs. We get out and head up to the front door. Nick doesn't bother knocking since the music is thumping so loud no one would hear it anyway. It's only nine o'clock, but it's clear this party's been going on for some time.

When we enter, it's a typical rich kid party. Tons of expensive liquor everywhere. Guys dressed in Lacoste, and girls donning Louis Vuitton and Burberry. Nick might've gone all big brother on me over the years, but that didn't stop me from finding my way into parties elsewhere, especially once he left last year for the NFL and couldn't keep tabs on me. I follow Nick over to the large dining room table where several guys are playing poker. Chips are stacked high and hundred-dollar bills are being thrown around like they're singles at a strip club.

When one of the guys spots Nick, he yells out his name, and everyone at the table stands to give Nick attention. I mentally roll my eyes. Nick is right about one thing: rich people are fake. But you know what else they are? Rich! I'll gladly take a fake, wealthy man over a heartfelt, poor one. Love doesn't pay the bills. Love doesn't have connections. These guys...they're the future of America. They'll graduate from college and follow in their rich daddy's footsteps, going on to work at Fortune 500 companies all over the world, and I'm going to snag one of them. Nick might've gotten me in the door with Elite, but that will only get me so far. Everyone knows money talks. My last name doesn't mean anything to anyone. But some of these guys...one mention of their name and I'll be heading straight to the top.

"How's it going?" Nick asks, greeting each of his friends, who are probably already thinking of how they can use their friendship with a famous quarterback to their advantage. Nick went into the NFL as a first-round draft pick as a backup quarterback. Due to the starting QB getting injured, he got a chance to show everyone what he's made of, and he soared. He took Carolina straight to the Super Bowl and won. Something that almost never happens with a first-year rookie.

"Jase!" Nick fist bumps his friend. "It's been too long, man."

His friend nods in agreement, but his eyes aren't on Nick—they're on me. And now, mine are on him. I take in his gelled ink-black hair, short enough not to be messy, but long enough I could run my fingers through it. His eyes, just as dark. Hard. Unforgiving. He's wearing a button-down white shirt with the sleeves rolled up to his elbows. I immediately spot several tattoos donning his muscular forearms. All shades of black and grey, no color. It's obvious, whoever this guy is, he isn't one of Nick's typical friends. He doesn't even try to suck up to Nick like the others do.

My eyes continue their perusal down his front. He's lean and, judging by the veins running down his forearms, he works out, but he's not a gym rat. He's wearing jeans that fit him just right and a pair of Nike's. Football player, maybe? The business majors usually wear Tom Ford or Brooks Brothers.

"And who's this?" Jase asks Nick with a knowing smirk. He's caught me checking him out.

"Just a friend of mine," Nick says dryly. When Jase clears his throat, indicating, not so subtly, he wants Nick to introduce us more thoroughly, Nick groans. "Celeste, this is Jase. We played ball together at Piermont Academy and at NCU. He was two years ahead of me." Hmm...so, he is a football player and a rich kid.

"Jase Crawford," Jase says, extending his hand. I give it willingly. "I'm pretty sure I've seen you on campus, but we've never formally met."

"Celeste is—" Nick begins, but I cut him off.

"...busy with school," I say, finishing Nick's sentence for him as I shake Jase's hand. There's no reason for Jase to know the *school* I'm busy with contains grades nine through twelve. I'm eighteen. That's all that matters.

Nick groans again, and I quickly shoot him a look that says if he groans one more damn time, I'll kill him.

"Nice." Jase grins, still holding my hand in his. "I graduated a couple years ago. Definitely don't miss the school work." Wealthy, educated, in shape, and hot as hell. I'm pretty sure I've just hit the jackpot.

"It's nice to meet you. How about you take a break from playing poker and get me a drink?" I bat my lashes, and Jase throws his head back with a laugh—one that has my insides melting like a pile of goo. What is wrong with me? I don't melt. I'm not that girl.

"All right," he says. "What would you like?" His lips curl up into a sexy smile.

"Something fruity would be great." My gaze stays glued to his mesmerizing mouth. His lips are full, and I try to imagine what it would feel like to kiss him.

"Got it." He lets go of my hand, and I miss it immediately. Jesus! Get a grip. He's just a guy. A rich guy who's hot and educated, but just a guy all the same. He went to Piermont Academy like Nick. He most likely comes from an influential family, and my goal is to see if he's someone I can use as a stepping stone to get me to where I want to go. Stick to the plan, Celeste!

When he walks away, Nick turns toward me. "Listen, Celeste, I know what you're thinking, but—"

"Nick, don't you dare cock-block me!" I say, cutting him off. "I swear to God, I will beat your ass," I hiss lowly, so no one can hear me.

Nick laughs. "One, you don't have a cock..."

"Fine! Vagina-block me," I cut in. "You know what I mean! Don't freaking block me!"

"Celeste, listen to me. Jase—"

"Jase!" I say a tad too loudly as I spot him walking back toward us. "That was quick." I take the drink he's holding out for me and take a sip. It's mostly liquor with a splash of...sprite? I choke down the burning sensation in my throat as I swallow. That...whatever it is... is definitely not fruity.

"Sorry." He cringes. "You took a sip before I could warn you. There wasn't anything fruity. The only thing close I could find was vodka and Sprite."

I let out a deep breath. "That's okay." I smile. "I love vodka." Nick laughs under his breath, knowing I'm lying through my teeth. I'm more of a rum girl...mixed into a fruity daiquiri.

"Celeste, can I talk to you for a minute?" Nick asks. My eyes swing over to him. I know he's protective of his friends, but he's never tried to block me like this, and I've gone on dates with a few of his college friends.

"Later, Nick," I say, trying to make it clear he needs to mind his own business.

He opens his mouth to speak again then closes it. Then his lips upturn into a wide smile and he says, "All right." He nods and laughs softly. "I'm going to play poker. You two enjoy yourselves." I'm not sure what made him suddenly change his disposition toward me going after Jase, but I'm not about to question it. Before Jase or I can say anything, one of the guys yells over at him to get his ass back to the poker table.

"Join me?" he asks. "You can be my good luck charm."

"Sure." I dramatically roll my eyes. "But you are aware every guy has at some point used that same line, right?"

Jase laughs. "I like you." Before he sits in his seat, he grabs another chair and pulls it next to him for me.

"All right, now that Nick is here, we can play a real

game," some guy says, throwing some more cash onto the table.

Nick chuckles. "Shut up, Ross. I'm on a damn rookie contract! Your allowance from your mommy and daddy probably pays more." The guys all laugh.

"Just deal," Jase says dryly. His hand lands on my thigh, and he leans into me. "All good luck charms have to do something to create the good luck." Before I can ask him what he's referring to, his lips meet mine. The kiss is soft and sweet, only lasting a brief moment. Yet in that short time, my entire body shivers in pleasure, my heart picks up speed, and if I wasn't sitting, my legs probably would've given out on me.

Jase pulls back and grants me a boyish grin. "Even if I lose, I'm considering that kiss getting lucky." His smile widens, and I release a giggle I didn't know I had in me at his cheesy flirting.

"Real smooth!" My hand smacks his shoulder playfully, and he grabs it, entwining our fingers together and bringing it up to his lips for a quick kiss before settling our hands in his lap. Nick eyes me warily, but I ignore him as I try to push away the butterflies which are currently fluttering in my belly. Nick might be worried about me destroying Jase, but right now, I'm more concerned about being the one to be destroyed.

I sip on my drink as the guys play. I've watched Nick play poker a few times with his friends when he lived on campus, but I don't know enough about the game to know who's winning. Several guys say they're out. Then the ones remaining lay their cards down flat for everybody to see.

"Hell yeah!" Jase cheers. He swipes all the chips toward him then turns in his chair to face me. "It's official, you're my good luck charm."

And without giving me any notice, he slants his mouth over mine. This time, the kiss is harder, more possessive, as if he's claiming me right here in front of everyone with this one kiss. Those fluttering butterflies are now attacking me as Jase's tongue pushes through my lips. He tastes of vodka and sprite, and it feels as if I could get drunk from this kiss alone. I can't help the small moan of pleasure that releases from my lips as his hand lands on my thigh and squeezes.

But just like the last kiss, this one also ends much too quickly, leaving me breathless and turned on, wanting, for the first time, more from a guy.

One of the guys says he's done and another guy takes his place, and then the cards are dealt. Everyone places their bets. Jase's hand finds my thigh, once again, and he gives it a soft squeeze.

My eyes find Nick's and he smirks. It's almost as if he knows I'm losing all my control to Jase. I don't know anything about him: does he have a trust fund? Where does his father work? Where does he work? What's his ten-year plan? But for some crazy reason, I don't seem to care about anything other than when his lips will find mine again.

Once again, I have no clue who's winning or losing, but it wouldn't matter because I can't focus. As Jase plays his hand of cards, his fingers run up and down my flesh, leaving a burning sensation in their wake. As his hand travels farther up, I clench my thighs together. He isn't going to do what I think he is...

He glances my way, asking for permission, and without even thinking twice I open my legs for him—*Jesus, when did I become so easy?* His fingers find my panties, but he doesn't move them to the side.

Instead, he teases me from the outside. His one finger trails up and down my slit through the thin material, and I squirm in my seat. I know I'm wet, probably drenched. There's no way anybody can know what he's doing, or see my reaction, yet I feel like all eyes are on us.

I can't believe I'm letting him do this. I don't even know this guy. For all I know, he does this with every girl he meets. I'm well aware everyone our age hooks up at parties, but that's never been who I am. Easy girls don't end up married to powerful men. They end up their mistresses.

Feeling like things are moving too quickly, I reach down and take his hand in mine. If he's annoyed I stopped him, he doesn't show it. He just continues to play poker one-handed like that's completely normal.

Jase wins for the third time, and the guys all groan. He leans over and presses his lips to mine. "One more hand and then I'm done," he murmurs against my mouth.

Before I back up, his tongue darts out and licks across my bottom lip. "Mmm...you taste good...sweet."

Less than ten minutes later, Jase wins. "I'm out," he announces as we stand. My eyes move to the front door, where I spot Killian Blake walking in. He glares my way, and I roll my eyes. Killian is Nick's *other* best friend. They met their freshman year of college. He's in his senior year at NCU and was recently drafted to the New York Brewers in the first round. To say we can't stand each other is a gross understatement. It's a good thing Jase is done playing poker and guiding me away from where Killian is walking toward. Had we stayed, I know, without a doubt, Killian would've made it a point to talk shit about me to Jase.

"So, you mentioned you recently graduated," I say to Jase, trying to get to know him as he pulls me toward the kitchen. Both of our cups are empty, so I'm assuming he's going to refill them.

"Yeah, I received my business degree." He takes my empty cup from me and sets it on the counter next to his. He drops a few ice cubes into both cups then pours some alcohol into them. Then he tops them off with a new can of sprite. "Cheers," he says, handing me my cup and taking a large drink from his own.

"Cheers," I say back. My sip is far smaller. Unlike Jase, who must be a good six feet tall, almost two hundred pounds, and clearly a seasoned drinker, my tiny one-hundred-and-ten-pound body can only handle so much alcohol before I'm drunk.

"Jase! Get your ass over here!" someone yells. "Drinking game!"

Jase laughs but shakes his head. "Nah, next time!"

"Now, bro," the guy demands. Jase gives me a look, silently asking if I mind. Not wanting to be the girl who takes him away from his friends, who he obviously came here tonight to see, I nod my okay.

"Fine, what game?" Jase yells over the music.

"Never have I ever!" a bleach-blonde girl shouts. I've seen her around NCU a few times, and I pray she doesn't ask me if I go there. "You in?" she asks me, not giving a shit about where I'm from.

"Sure." I hold up my drink.

Everyone goes around the room calling out things they've never done, and those who've done them have to drink:

Gotten wasted—most drink

Stolen their parent's car—a few drink

Went skinny-dipping—most drink

Smoked weed—almost everyone drinks

Had a three-some—only a couple drink

And then some girl yells through a fit of drunken laughter, "Had sex." I watch as everyone around me drinks and laughs at her because she's just announced that she's still a virgin. Until she joins in with everyone else and downs her drink. "Whoops! My bad!" She laughs harder.

Jase's eyes go to mine, and I realize I haven't taken a

drink. I tip my cup back and take a large gulp. He smiles and raises his cup in a 'cheers' motion, so I do the same.

The questions continue for a little while longer, but when Jase notices that I've run out of alcohol, he excuses us from the game. We head out the back door and onto the patio. There are people out here, but not as many.

With the door closed, the music is now muffled, allowing us to hear each other better. We walk down the dock and find an empty spot on the beach. In contrast to the warm weather we've been having lately, it's a bit chilly tonight, but luckily there's hardly any breeze. In an attempt to look good, I didn't think to bring a jacket.

Jase, the gentleman he is, shrugs out of his and drapes it across my shoulders. "Thank you." I smile over at him. "I was clearly going for sexy and not practical." My words are a tad slurred from the drinking I've been doing, and we both laugh.

"Well, you did sexy to perfection," he says, sitting down on the damp sand.

I eye it, afraid my dress will get ruined or my butt will end up frozen. But before I can make the decision whether to sit, Jase pulls me into his lap. My dress rises, and I'm thankful we're in the dark because my panties are definitely on display. I'm straddling his thighs with my legs wrapped around him—the tips of my wedges are resting in the sand. Alarm bells should be going off in my head. This is all happening too fast. But all I can focus on is the way his strong hands grip my hips. The feel of his lips—strong yet soft—as they work their way down the side of my neck and over to my throat. My fingers run through his hair as he trails soft kisses down my throat. I relish in the delicious friction our bodies are creating as my butt grinds against his pelvis.

The sound of police sirens ring through the air, and Jase stops what he's doing, his eyes locking with mine. "I've had too much to drink to drive," he says. "Let me call my brother." With me still sitting on his lap, he pulls his phone out of his pocket and dials a number. "Jax, it's me. I need you to come get me from Jared's. The cops have been called." There's a pause. "I've been drinking." Another pause. "Thanks, bro. I'll meet you down by the south pier." He hangs up, and lifting me off him like I weigh nothing, stands me on my feet.

"I came with Nick," I point out. "He wouldn't leave without me."

"Call him and let him know that I'm dropping you off," Jase says, walking us down the beach toward the pier. I do as he says and call Nick. He answers on the first ring. When I tell him Jase is going to drop me off, he points out he's been drinking and insists on finding me. But when I tell him his brother is coming to get us, Nick concedes, but makes me promise to text him as soon as I'm home.

When Jase's brother shows up, Jase opens the door for me to get into the front seat. Once I'm in, he climbs into the back. "Quinn grabbed your car," Jax says. "She's meeting us back at home."

"Thanks, bro."

"I'm Jax," Jase's brother says, introducing himself.

"I'm Celeste. Thank you for getting us."

"No worries. Where am I taking you?"

Jase's hand lands on my shoulder, and he squeezes softly. Then his cool breath is at my ear. "Come home with me," he whispers.

My body thrums at the thought of spending more time with Jase, of our night not coming to an end just yet. I've never spent the night with a guy before, and while it makes me somewhat nervous, I remember that Nick is friends with him, and he wouldn't have introduced us, or let Jase and his brother take me home, if he was worried something would happen to me. For a few seconds I weigh my options, but ultimately my need to spend more time with Jase wins out.

I nod once. "Okay."

"Just take us back to our place," Jase tells his brother.

We arrive at their apartment, and just as I suspected, it's in a nicer part of town. The apartment itself isn't huge, but it's clean and decorated beautifully. When we walk inside, a gorgeous woman is standing against the island, drinking a bottle of water. She's wearing a cute grey hoodie and matching tiny shorts that show off her thick, toned legs. At a second glance, I spot a few colorful tattoos peeking out from under her shorts. Her jet-black hair is down in waves, and her face is free of all makeup. She throws a set of keys at Jase. "You're welcome."

Jase gives her a simple chin lift. "Thanks." He puts his arm around my shoulders and pulls me into his side. "Celeste, this is my baby sister, Quinn."

"Baby?" She scoffs. "I'm a whole five years younger." She rolls her eyes.

"You're nineteen. A baby," Jase argues, and I stiffen. If she's a baby in his eyes, he would throw my ass out if he knew I'm only eighteen. Sure, I'm legal, but I'm a good six years younger than him.

"And yet, I'm the one playing the parent by picking up your vehicle because you're out partying." She snorts.

"Yeah, yeah, we're going to bed," Jase calls over his shoulder as he walks us away from the kitchen and down the hall. When we get to the last door on the right, he opens the door so I can walk through first, then closes it behind him.

Suddenly I'm nervous. I never imagined I would end up here with Jase—or any guy for that matter. I attend parties for the sole purpose of finding myself a wealthy guy to take me to dinner, to use as a contact. Men have never been anything more than a potential stepping stone to me. Until now. I knew what I was agreeing to when I said okay to coming back here. I know what the people our age do when they go back to each other's places, but it didn't hit me until this very moment that, for the first time, *I've* agreed to go back to a guy's place. And surprisingly, while I am nervous, I'm not scared, and I don't regret saying okay. "I better text Nick to let him know I'm here," I tell him.

"Okay." He shrugs. "I'm going to change." He pulls some clothes from his drawer and hands them to me. "So you're more comfortable."

"Thank you."

I pull my phone out of my bra, where I keep it when I have no pockets, and am about to text Nick to tell him where I am, when something stops me. It's not like Jase is going to murder me here. He lives with his brother and sister. He played high school and college ball with Nick. If I text Nick where I am, I'll never hear the end of it. So, instead, I text him that I made it home safely, and he, none the wiser, texts back that he'll see me tomorrow.

I change out of my dress and peel off my wedges, then I throw on the clothes Jase gave me—a shirt and boxers. The masculine, fresh scent of him hits my senses, and my only thought is *my god, he smells good.*

Not having a hair tie on me, but wanting to get my hair off my neck, I twist and pull it all up into a makeshift bun and tie it using my hair. While I wait for him to come out from his attached bathroom, I take a slow stroll around his room. It's a guy's room. Simple for the most part. Plain wood dresser, matching nightstands. A large king size bed with a simple black comforter. But the walls are another story. Each one is filled with beautiful hand-drawn art. Some are shades of black, white, and grey, and others are vivid colors that pop out as if the images are coming to life. One of his walls looks like it's been graffitied, but it's too pretty to call it that.

Jase comes back into the room as I'm staring at one of the pictures on his walls. It's a wolf that looks to be morphing into some kind of scary-looking skeleton. "This is...amazing," I tell him. "Did you draw all these?"

When he doesn't answer, I look over at him. He's leaning against the dresser, his hands in the pockets of his sweatpants, staring at me like he wants to devour me. "You look sexy as hell in my clothes," he says, his eyes dragging down my body. I swallow thickly at his statement. I'm so far out of my comfort zone here. With him now in a short-sleeved T-shirt, more of his tattoos are on display. They cover most of the skin on his arms. I wonder if he has any on his chest or his back. I bet he does.

Without saying another word, Jase stalks toward me and presses me against the wall. His hands find mine, and he pushes them over my head, my wrists making a thumping sound as they hit the wall. My mind goes foggy with lust as I get lost in this man's touch. His knee parts my thighs and grinds against my core, forcing a shudder of pleasure from me. Then his hands release mine, and he grips my hips, lifting me.

My legs wrap around his waist as he carries me to the bed, dropping me onto the middle of the mattress. He climbs on top of me, his lips immediately finding mine. We kiss hard as his hand cups and massages my breast. I squirm under his touch. I've never felt like this before. This turned on. This reckless. All of my man-goals have flown out the window.

Without breaking our kiss, Jase pushes the boxers I'm wearing down my thighs along with my panties. Alarms of warning sound off, but they're too faint to pay attention to. My brain is too hazy. My judgement is too clouded. I want him. Bad. Jase's hand pushes my thighs apart and his fingers enter me. "Fuck, you're wet," he murmurs against my lips. I can't speak. I can't respond. All I can do is moan in pleasure as he fingers me. His thumb finds my clit and massages slow circles over the tight, swollen nub.

Ending our kiss, he dips his head down, and with his nose, pushes my shirt up, trailing kisses up my stomach. I pull my shirt the rest of the way over my head and throw it to the side. My bra is still on, but my nipples have pebbled through the thin material. He kisses then sucks on each one, leaving a wet spot where his mouth was.

"Your tits are fucking perfect," he murmurs as he lowers one of the cups and wraps his perfect lips around the hardened bud. And then he bites down—hard—and that's all it takes for my orgasm to rip through my body.

Before I can catch my breath, Jase is reaching back and pulling his shirt over his head. I only have a moment to appreciate the work of art that is his body before he pushes his sweatpants down, forcing my gaze to leave his tattoo-covered chest and go lower. Gripping his thick shaft in his hand, he strokes it once, twice, and then in one fluid motion, enters me.

I could've stopped him. But I didn't. The pain tears

through me. Not wanting to scream, my mouth finds his shoulder, and I bite down. The act spurs him on, and he thrusts deeper into me, pushing through the barrier of my virginity. Then he stills as if he felt it.

"Celeste," he whispers. He's about to pull out. I can feel it. But before he does, I lock my ankles around his backside.

"Keep going," I plead. His head lifts, and his eyes meet mine. They're dark and filled with regret. "Please," I beg. His eyes squeeze shut as he wars with himself. It's too late now. He's already taken my virginity. "Please," I repeat. My hands come up to his head, and I tug on his hair, pulling his face toward mine. My lips fuse against his. Without opening his eyes, he kisses me back and thrusts into me again. This time, though, it's slower, gentler. He knows. One of his hands cradles the side of my head while the other comes down between us, landing on my clit.

Jase continues to fuck me, but I'm not sure if what he's doing can even be called fucking. It's more like he's making love to me, only it can't be called making love either. We barely know each other. You can't love someone you barely know. He works me up once again, and before I know it, I'm climaxing for a second time with Jase following right behind.

We both still as we catch our breath. Jase's head falls onto my chest, and I feel his thick lashes flutter against my over-sensitive flesh. He lets out a groan and shakes his head. I'm afraid to say anything. I should've told him I was a virgin. That's on me. He lifts off of me as he pulls out, taking his warmth with him. His eyes go wide as he looks down. My gaze follows his, and that's when I see it. Blood covering his still semi-hard length, proving what he was probably hoping wasn't true.

He stands, and without saying a word, heads into his bathroom. I'm stuck, frozen in place, unsure what I should do now. I need to clean up. And that's when it hits me. We didn't use protection. I'm on birth control, but that's beside the point. I consider joining him in the bathroom but wonder if that would be too intimate. Should I wait for him to get out and then haul my ass inside? Before I can figure out what to do, Jase exits the bathroom carrying a washcloth. He spreads my legs and wipes down my center—the cream-colored material turns crimson.

He tosses it into his hamper and grabs a new pair of boxers for himself. Then he picks the shirt I was wearing up off the floor and hands it to me. I thank him and shrug it on, barely making eye contact. I think he's going to hand me back my panties or his boxers, but he doesn't. Instead, he crawls into bed next to me and pulls me into his body until our fronts are almost flush against each other.

"You should've told me," he murmurs, pushing my hair out of my face.

"I'm sorry," I whisper back, feeling completely embarrassed.

"I should've used a condom. I know it's going to

sound cliché as fuck, but I *always* use one. I don't know what the hell got into me." I flinch at his words, but try to hide it. I'd rather not think about all the other women he's been with.

"I'm on birth control," I admit softly.

We lay together in silence for a few minutes, and then Jase murmurs, "I've never felt anything like this. I've been with my fair share of women, but I've never felt this connection. I know we've only just met, but tell me you feel it too."

I nod in agreement. It's crazy to feel the way I do. To let this guy I barely know take my virginity. There's a good chance I'm going to regret it tomorrow, but right now, it feels right.

"Tell me something about you," he says, his lips curling into a beautiful, lazy smile. "But first, what's your last name?"

I laugh. We're obviously doing this all backwards. "My last name is Leblanc."

"And..."

"And I want to be a model," I admit. It's the only thing I can think of that won't scare him away. My age, where I go to school, where I live...it's all off limits.

Jase smirks. "You're definitely beautiful enough. What kind of model?" He takes my fingers in his hand and brings them to his lips for a kiss. "A hand model? Because you have seriously sexy fingers." He sucks my middle finger into his mouth erotically, and a soft moan escapes my lips. How can something as simple as him sucking on my finger turn me on?

"No," I croak, then clear my throat before I continue. "A real model." I gently pull my finger out from between his lips. "My dream is to be on billboards across New York. I want to walk the catwalks for high fashion designers during the New York, Paris, and Milan Fashion Weeks. I want to get a deal with Victoria's Secret or Tommy Hilfiger, or maybe Donna Karen or Chanel." I can't help the excitement I feel when I talk about my goals and dreams. Growing up, I used to toy with the idea of wanting to become a model. I would play dress up with Nick's mom's clothes when she wasn't home, and force Nick to watch me put on fashion shows.

When I got older, I would watch the various fashion shows on television when Mom remembered to pay the bill. But it was confirmed the first time Nick's mom brought Nick and me along with her for Fashion Week when I was twelve years old. Nick's nanny got sick and canceled last minute, and his dad was out of town on business. Like always, my mom was in a drunken stupor, so Victoria ended up taking us with her to New York.

She was able to find a replacement nanny for the rest of the week, but that first night we went with her, and it was that one night that changed my life. Up until that day, my dreams were puffs of clouds in the sky—beautiful to look up at, but unreachable. But as I watched the fashion show from the third row, it was as if I was floating in the air. I could taste it, smell it, feel it. For the first time, my dreams were within reach, and I knew I would do everything in my power to grab ahold of them.

"But I don't want to stop there," I continue when I see Jase's eyes are on me, that he's actually listening and waiting for me to explain. I can't remember the last time someone just listened to me. "It's common knowledge that a modeling career peaks by twenty-two and is over by twenty-seven, thirty, if the model is lucky. Modeling is my dream, my foot in the door, but I don't want that to be it. I want to start my own jewelry and makeup lines. Maybe even a clothing line. I love fashion," I exclaim.

"Why?" he asks thoughtfully.

"I love the way an outfit can give a woman confidence. The way makeup can make her feel beautiful. I love how a single necklace or bracelet can make her feel... more." I don't know how to explain it without telling him I was raised in a shitty trailer park, in an ugly, tiny trailer. I grew up being made fun of for wearing the Walmart clothes my mom would buy me secondhand from the thrift stores. The no-name brand shoes that she would pick up from the local consignment shops. Kids were mean, and I always felt so ugly.

That was until Nick's mom, Victoria, bought me a beautiful Marc Jacobs gown for the function we were attending. She took me to get my hair and makeup and nails done. Then she lent me a pair of pearl earrings and a matching necklace.

That night, not only did nobody make fun of me, but I was complimented on several occasions on how beautiful I looked. I watched the models strut up and down the runway as everybody oohed and ahhed, and it was in that moment I knew I would do whatever it took to become a model. I want to travel the world, wear gorgeous, expensive clothes, get paid to put on makeup. I want to live in a penthouse that overlooks Central Park. I want a husband who's rich and takes care of me and thinks I'm beautiful.

Jase eyes me curiously and then says, "You don't need to do anything to make yourself beautiful. You already are." We've only just met, yet it's as if he has the ability to read the words I'm not saying. Say the things I long for someone to say. Tears sting my eyes, and I force them away.

"What about you?" I ask, my throat clogged with emotion. "What do you want to be?"

"I want to open my own tattoo shop." His answer should be the equivalent of ice being thrown onto my overheated body. *A tattoo shop.* That's hardly a fortune 500 company. He's nothing like the wealthy husband I envisioned for myself. But for some reason, I don't care. Instead, his answer makes me smile. I can totally see it. The drawings all over his walls, the gorgeous ink covering his body. The dark aura that surrounds him. It all fits.

"Is that why you majored in business?"

He nods. "Yeah, Jax and I both have our licenses to

tattoo, but he wasn't able to go to college. We didn't have the money." He frowns, appearing to be embarrassed. "I got a football scholarship to attend NCU and figured it would do us good for me to learn how to run a business." He grants me a soft smile. "Now we just have to save up."

"Didn't you go to Piermont Academy with Nick?" I ask, confused. He's clearly not from a family with money and that school is over fifty thousand a year alone just for the tuition.

"Yeah, another scholarship." He shrugs one shoulder. "My brother went to Piermont Public."

"Your sister?" She's only a year ahead of me, but I've never seen her at school.

"Piermont Academy on an academic scholarship. She's now attending The Art Institute. Between her financial aid, and Jax and me helping her, we're handling it okay." He flinches at his own words, telling me there's more to it than him and his brother handling it. Is it possible he comes from a home like mine? One where your parent doesn't handle shit? I want to open up to him, but if I do, he'll find out I'm not in college and that I'm younger than I led him to believe, and there's no way he won't push me away.

"Does she want to do tattoos like you and your brother?" Absentmindedly, my hand finds its way to Jase's scalp, and I thread my fingers through his thick hair. It's like I need to touch him in some way at all times. He must feel the same, because as we talk, his hand, the one that isn't trapped under me and gripping my hip, roams over my body.

"No, she's more about the traditional type of art. She loves photography, graphic design, sculpting." The way he speaks about his sister, it's obvious he's proud of her.

Jase's gaze drops to my mouth, and he dips his head down to snag my lower lip, pulling it roughly and sucking on my flesh. "We should get some sleep. I'm on the verge of wanting to take you again, and I imagine you're sore."

Before I can respond, his lips find mine, deliciously contradicting his words. This kiss is soft and sweet, and when it ends, I sigh in need. Jase chuckles under his breath before rolling onto his back and pulling me into his side.

No words are spoken.

No promises of tomorrow.

Instead, we remain in the present, falling asleep in each other's arms.

Chapter Three

CELESTE
THE PAST

I WAKE UP TO THE FEELING OF... WELL, I'M NOT quite sure what it is. Something is tickling my back. My eyes open, and it only takes a second to remember where I am. At Jase's place in his bed. I'm lying on my belly, only Jase is no longer my human pillow—albeit a firm one. The light glaring in through the blind slats have my eyes closing. My hand reaches out blindly for Jase, but his side of the bed is empty. That's when I feel it again. The tickling on my back. *Oh, God, please don't let it be a bug or an animal...* I'm about to turn over to see what it is, but a strong hand weighing down on my butt prevents me from moving.

"Don't move," Jase's husky voice says. "I'm almost done." Twisting my head without moving the rest of my body, I peek behind me and see the tickling is Jase drawing on my skin.

"Are you drawing on me?"

"I couldn't help it. Your body is flawless..." The hand that was on my butt, cups my cheek and then slides down the back of my thigh. "Like a blank canvas, just waiting for its story." Goosebumps prickle my skin at his words as I wonder if my story will include him.

"You were sleeping so soundly, and when I woke up to take a piss, I noticed my shirt had risen, exposing this sexy ass" —he trails his hand back up my thigh and gives my backside a playful slap— "and these perfect dimples." My head falls forward onto the pillow. His cool lips graze my lower back as he gives the two dimples located just above my ass a kiss.

"I had to mark you," he adds, and my eyes flit over to him again. He's back to drawing on me while he talks. "You know, I've done quite a few dimple piercings. Do you have any piercings?"

"No." I shake my head.

"Tattoos?"

"Nope. Piercings and tattoos are a no-no when you're trying to become a model. Most high-class agencies frown upon that sort of thing."

Jase grunts his displeasure, continuing to draw on my body. "Nobody would know if you got one here," he states. His fingers trail down to just above the crack of my ass. "Or here." He continues his descent along the center of my ass. Then he spreads my legs open and pushes a single finger into my pussy. "Nobody should ever see these parts of your body. They're mine," he growls lowly. "This body, and this pussy, is mine." He pulls his finger out of me, and I immediately miss his touch.

"It's a little soon to be claiming me, don't you think?" I sass.

"Nope, you made it mine the moment you let me take your virginity," he says matter-of-factly, and my cheeks flush at his words.

"Don't move," he demands. He pushes off the bed, and a second later, I hear the sound of a camera clicking. "Perfect."

I try to flip over, but his hands prevent me from doing so. Jase spreads my thighs wider and pushes his fingers back inside me, my body accepting the intrusion all too willingly.

"Jesus, woman, you're so wet," he groans.

While he fingers me with one hand, his other comes around and lifts my lower half slightly off the bed, so I'm on my knees. He palms my breast and plants sweet kisses down my spine until his lips are back where he was drawing. He blows softly on my skin, sending chills up my spine. Then his lips once again kiss each of my dimples. He makes his way downward, and when his teeth sink into my butt cheek, I let out a girly screech.

He laughs softly. "Sorry, I needed a taste," he admits, and I can't help the grin that makes its way across my face in response.

He continues to fingerfuck me, and then his tongue

hits my clit. He sucks it into his mouth and then licks up my center, causing my entire body to shudder in pleasure. With his tongue, and lips, and fingers, Jase works me up until I'm calling out his name as I orgasm around him.

Then he flips me over onto my back and crawls up my body. My legs wrap around his waist as his hands cage me in. His lips angle against mine as he pushes into me. I'm still a tad sore, but those thoughts are overpowered by our kiss.

This kiss. It ignites something deep within me, heating my frozen walls and melting the ice away until there's nothing left to protect my heart and soul. They're visible and vulnerable, leaving Jase with full access to every exposed part of me. Our kiss becomes more heated. Like a wildfire that can't be contained. I've always been so careful—never to let anyone in. Yet, here I am, handing myself over to this man, knowing if I'm not careful, I'm going to get burned. The heat between us is all-consuming. I'm lost in everything that is Jase.

My hands hold on to his shoulders, my nails digging into his skin, as his thrusts turn frantic. His pelvis grinds against mine, rubbing my clit just right. We're both chasing our release. My climax builds, and builds, and builds, until I'm so high, I have nowhere to go but down. But with Jase in charge, I'm not afraid to fall. In fact, I welcome it. And with one last thrust, he pushes me off the edge, taking himself with me. Our lips find each other, swallowing our moans as we both lose ourselves in one another.

Once we've reached the bottom safely, Jase breaks our kiss and nuzzles his face into the crook of my neck. We stay like this for a long moment as we calm our beating hearts and labored breaths. When he lifts slightly, pulling out, I wince at the tenderness I feel between my legs, hoping I never stop feeling it, so I always remember the times Jase and I became one.

"Shit, I didn't use protection *again*," he admits, looking down. It's then I feel the liquid between my thighs *again*. I should be bothered that Jase and I have yet to use protection. I know this is a one-night stand. But for some crazy reason, being with Jase feels like so much more.

"It's okay," I blurt out, "I trust you."

Jase pulls my face into his for a hard kiss. "What are you doing to me?" he murmurs against my lips. "All my sanity flies out the window with you."

"Because you forgot to use a condom?" I ask, confused.

"I never bring women back here. Not to my apartment, not to meet my family, and definitely not into my bed."

"I should get cleaned up," I tell him shyly, not completely sure what to say in response to his admission. His words have my insides on fire, my heart thumping in my chest. But I just met him not even twelve hours ago. I don't have any other relationships to compare this to, but I can't imagine falling for someone this fast is the norm.

Jase backs up so I can climb off the bed. Following

me into his bathroom, he insists we shower together. I've never showered with a man before, but Jase doesn't make me feel the slightest bit uncomfortable. The entire time we're in the shower, he makes it a point to touch me in some way. Whether it's soaping me up, or massaging the shampoo into my scalp, his hands are on me. And the more he touches me, gives me his undivided attention, the more I want to stay in our little bubble and never leave.

When we get out, he tells me he'll be right back. He returns with a pair of sweats and a hoodie. They're pink and similar to the outfit Quinn was wearing.

"Thank you. I'll wash them and then get them back to her."

I pull my hair up into a messy bun then get dressed. I put my bra back on but go commando, not wanting to wear my day-old panties. I gather up my clothes from last night and fold them into a neat pile while Jase gets dressed.

My heart tightens in my chest when I hear the clinking of his keys. This is it. Our night together is over. He's going to take me home, and then he'll continue his life while I continue mine. Tears prick my eyes, and I quickly lift my finger to wipe them away. I don't cry. Why am I crying now? Grow up, Celeste! This is what people our age do. We have one-night stands. We hook up and then go our separate ways. Don't act like an immature weirdo.

"I almost forgot to show you," Jase says, breaking me

out of my crazy silent monologue. I take a deep breath and turn to face him. He's dressed in a plain white T-shirt that stretches across his broad chest and shoulders, and a loose pair of jeans. His one arm comes up so his fingers can run through his damp hair, and I spot a hint of his thick happy trail leading down to the Promised Land. I should've spent more time getting to know his body while I had him. I didn't even have a chance to taste him yet.

Jase clears his throat, and it's then I notice he's facing his phone toward me and sporting a knowing smirk. He totally caught me checking him out. I simply shrug. No point in denying it. I step closer to see what's on his screen and immediately recognize the one dimple on my lower back.

And then my focus turns to the most beautiful artwork I've ever seen. A black and grey dandelion that looks like it's blowing in the wind comes up my hip with stray petals dancing in the wind. A smaller one next to it. Along the stem of the larger dandelion is a quote: *And from the chaos of her soul flowed beauty.*

"Jase," I whisper. How could he possibly write something that hits so close to home without even knowing me? Understand the chaos that I feel deep inside of me every day? The confusion that flows through me when I think about where I come from and where I want to go. The struggle to love myself but at the same time want more.

"My mom used to wish on dandelions," Jase says, his

voice thick with emotion. "She would take Jax and me for walks in our neighborhood when we were little, and she would find every single one she could, blowing on them as she made wish after wish."

"What did she wish for?"

"I don't know." He shrugs a shoulder. "But my guess is success. She wanted to be an actress." He smiles warmly. "She was beautiful. At least from what I can remember." The corners of his mouth turn down slightly. "She was actually in a couple small shows, but then she met my dad. She fell in love and found herself pregnant with my brother. A year later came me." I notice he doesn't mention Quinn. "She didn't know it at the time, but my dad was already married. His wife couldn't have kids...or so they thought. A few years later, Quinn was born.

"My dad juggled his two families for a while, but eventually he got caught. When his wife found out about us, he proved my mom to be an unfit parent and got custody of us. My mom couldn't handle it—losing my dad and us. She had given up her dreams for him, only to learn he didn't feel the same way about her. She ended up committing suicide."

"Oh, Jase!" My arms wrap around his neck for a hug. "I'm so sorry."

"You remind me of her," Jase murmurs into my ear. "I saw that quote captioned under an image at an art gallery I visited once with my sister. I can't remember who said it, but the words always stuck with me. I don't doubt one day you will conquer the world, Dimples." He backs up and shoots me a playful wink to lighten the mood, but my heart is still with Jase's mom and her chaotic, beautiful soul.

"Where's your dad now?" I ask. He obviously accepted Quinn as his sister even though she has a different mom.

"He died of a heart attack when I was thirteen." Jase doesn't sound the least bit sad when he tells me this. "Quinn's mom thought she would get his life insurance, but it came out that he wasn't really married to her either. He was married to another woman, Tricia, and had two other kids with her. He had left her several years back but never got a divorce. She got everything in his will, leaving Quinn's mom broke. She lost her shit, and the minute Jax turned eighteen, he got a job and moved out. He petitioned the court and got custody of Quinn. I was already almost eighteen, so the judge approved for me to become emancipated."

"Wow," I say in awe of how well they handled everything.

"Yeah, talk about some crazy 60 Minutes meets Jerry Springer shit." Jase laughs humorlessly. "My dad was a fucking liar, and his lies destroyed not one but two women who loved him." He shakes his head with disgust. "I hope he's rotting in hell." His words hit me like a brick to a glass house. Jase's hard limit is lying, and I've lied to him several times since we met. No, I didn't actually say the words, but I might as well have. I should tell him the truth now. What do I have to lose? But if I walk away with things the way they are now, he won't think of me the way he thinks about his father. As a liar.

My eyes dart to his phone, the screen is still showing the fake tattoo he drew on me. "Can you send me that picture?" I ask. It's the only thing I will have left of our night together once I walk away.

"Sure." He grins. I give him my email address since my phone is one of those crappy prepaid ones, and he sends it over.

We walk out of his room and find Jax cooking in the kitchen with Quinn sitting on a stool watching him. "Morning," Jase announces. Jax and Quinn both glance our way. Quinn grants me a soft smile, and Jax waves the spatula in the air.

"Morning," they both say in unison.

"You hungry?" Jax asks.

"Starving!" I admit before I can stop myself. Jase is probably ready to send me packing, and I'm over here practically begging to stay and eat.

"Well, have a seat." Jax points to the empty stools.

"Oh, umm...I think Jase was about to take me home." I avoid looking at anyone in the room, instead choosing to focus on the pancake batter that's bubbling in the pan. It's embarrassing enough having to do the walk of shame...

The contrast between the coolness of Jase's lips on my ear, and his warm body pressed up against mine, sends a visible shiver straight down my spine. He must notice because he chuckles softly before he says, "You aren't going anywhere, Dimples. Sit." I do as he says, while trying to school my excitement over his somewhat public display of affection and sweet yet commanding words, but a grin stretches across my lips anyway.

Quinn laughs. "Such a gentleman," she jokes.

"Hush your mouth," Jase volleys back.

Jax serves us each a stack of delicious-smelling pancakes and eggs then has a seat as well.

"What's everyone up to today?" Quinn asks.

"I have a guy coming into the shop to get more of his sleeve done," Jax says.

"What about you guys?" Quinn turns her attention to Jase and me.

"Not sure yet," Jase answers her. The hand he's not using to eat squeezes my thigh. I assumed Jase was going to bring me home, yet he told me I'm not going anywhere. Did he just mean to stay for breakfast? We haven't discussed what happened between us last night, and for all I know this was just a one-night thing to him.

At least that's what I keep telling myself when I justify why I haven't told him the truth about my age and where I go to school. Maybe he just plans to fill my belly with food before he sends me on my way.

"I'm heading to the beach to take pictures," Quinn says. "I have my final photography project due next week."

Jase swallows a mouthful of food, then turns to me. "Want to go?" The look he gives me is so hopeful. Before

I can think about the ramifications of my answer, I'm nodding my head yes. He smiles an adorable lopsided grin. "Cool. We can go by your house to get your suit on the way."

Shit! This is exactly why I should've given this more thought before saying yes. I need to tell him the truth. He needs to know I'm only eighteen and in high school. That I live in a trailer park with my drunken mother, and my only way out is the summer internship in New York Nick surprised me with. Jase would understand. He comes from a broken home. And I am of legal age...

I open my mouth to tell Jase I need to talk to him, when Quinn says, "I have a spare." She shrugs. "It'll save time."

"You good with that?" Jase asks, taking another bite of his food.

"Yeah," I mutter with a plastered-on smile. *Later... I'll tell him later.*

Once we're done eating, and we've worked together to get the dishes done and the kitchen cleaned, we head out in Jase's Dodge Charger to the beach. It's such a man's car. Black on black with smooth, leather interior. It's not flashy or expensive, but it's damn sexy. And it totally fits him.

When we arrive at the beach, Quinn takes off on her photography mission, and Jase and I head toward the ocean to find an empty spot to lay a blanket down near the water.

After stripping off Quinn's shirt and shorts, leaving me in only her bikini—which fits a tad loose on my body since she has more curves than I do—I turn my attention to Jase. He reaches back and pulls his shirt over his head, exposing his delicious tattoos, along with his firm chest and ripped abs. I never imagined falling for a guy like Jase. I always pictured a wealthy, put together businessman, dressed to the nines in a designer suit. Nowhere in my fantasies did it include a tattoo artist bad-boy. The term causes my heart to skip a beat. My mom fell for the tattooed bad-boy. She's not only brokenhearted but *broken*. *It's not the same*, I tell myself. Jase isn't really a bad-boy. He just looks like one. He's educated. He has a college degree, and he wants to open his own business.

Does it really even matter when this time next week I'll be in New York?

My heart sinks at the thought of leaving Jase. Can I do it? Can I walk away from him?

You don't have a choice, my inner self argues. It doesn't matter how fast and hard I'm falling for him. New York is my future. I can't give that up for a *man*. There will be plenty more men in New York.

"You okay?" Jase asks, forcing me out of my thoughts.

"Yeah," I say, and then quickly add, "tell me about your tattoos," in hope of distracting myself from my own thoughts. My mind and heart are warring with one another, and it's not a battle I'm ready to enter yet.

Jase looks down and runs a hand along the planes

of his abs. "Which ones?" he asks. "I kind of have a lot." He laughs, and the melodic sound calms my nerves. No, he's not a bad-boy. He's a good guy wrapped in a bad-boy body.

He drops onto the blanket and lays next to me. His leg entangles with mine as he explains each one. They all mean something to him in some way. We spend the next several hours laughing and talking and kissing, completely lost in our own little world. We watch people come and go, and eat the lunch we packed. The water is warm, so we go swimming as well. Eventually Quinn makes her way back over to us, ready to go home. I have no clue how the entire day passed so quickly, but what I do know is I'm not ready to say goodbye to Jase yet.

So when he murmurs, "Come home with me" against my lips, I agree without thought. On our drive back, Nick texts, asking where I am. I text him back that I have a couple things I need to do before graduation, immediately feeling guilty for lying. But I'm not ready for him to know about Jase yet. It's pointless for him to know about a man I can't have a future with. It's not like I'm going to stay. And on top of that, I lied to Jase. Sure, they're technically lies by omission, but a lie is still a lie. He doesn't even know I'm planning to leave soon.

Jase's hand squeezes mine, and my heart feels like it's going to thump right out of my chest. How did this happen? How did I manage to fall for someone this fast? This isn't who I am. I want to be mad at myself for being so stupid, but I can't muster up the negative energy. My heart feels too full...too happy. And suddenly I can almost empathize with my mom. Imagining how I'm going to feel when I leave next week nearly has my heart crumbling into pieces.

Grabbing our stuff, we head upstairs to their apartment. Jase unlocks the door and opens it wide for Quinn and me to walk through. I stop in my place when I see a woman sitting on the couch, fiddling with her cell phone. I glance around and don't see Jax anywhere. Does she live here as well?

She looks up, and it's as if she doesn't even notice Quinn or me in the room as she smiles at Jase. She's naturally beautiful with fiery red hair and emerald green eyes, but she looks exhausted—like she has the weight of the world sitting on her shoulders. Her eyes then dart to me, and she glares daggers my way. When her gaze goes back to Jase, her smile comes back. *Interesting...*

"Jase!" She jumps off the couch and flies into his arms. His eyes meet mine, and he shoots me, what looks like, a silent apology. The woman is dressed in black jeans that are clearly too tight on her, and a tiny blue tank top. A large tattoo peeks out from under her shirt on her lower back, disappearing under the top of her jeans. And a twinge of jealousy surfaces as I wonder if Jase was the one to give it to her.

"Amaya," he says, pulling away from her. "How are you?" His eyes trails down her body, not like he's checking her out, but more like he's making sure she's okay.

"I'm fine," she says a bit too upbeat. It reminds me of the way my mom speaks to Victoria to hide how drunk she is, or when she doesn't want her to know we're without electric or water. "Are you going to introduce me to your friend?" She nods my way. "Or is she Quinn's friend?" she adds, hope evident in her voice.

"She's with Jase," Quinn says matter-of-factly to the woman, and I bite down on my bottom lip to stifle a smile. Quinn just got major points for that in my book.

"This is Celeste," Jase says, then turns toward me. "This is my friend, Amaya."

"Best friend," Amaya corrects with a bit of snark in her tone.

"Nice to meet you," I say politely. "I'm going to shower the sand and ocean off me." I give Jase a soft smile, so he knows I'm trying to be nice and leave them to talk. She's obviously here for a reason.

"Bye!" Amaya waves at me like she's five years old.

Jase shoots her a cool glare, then mouths a *thank you* to me.

I LET OUT A SOFT SIGH AS THE HOT WATER rains down and massages my scalp. My eyes are closed so the shampoo doesn't burn them as the water rinses the suds and salt from my hair. I'm completely lost in myself, in my thoughts, so I don't hear Jase come in. When the shower door opens, and the cool air pricks my heated flesh, I let out a loud shriek. Jase laughs, but when his eyes land on my now pebbled nipples, his laughter stops, and the smile he was just sporting turns into pure hunger.

"Get in or get out! It's cold out there!" I yell, trying to sound mad. A laugh breaks through, though, giving me away.

Jase steps in and closes the door behind him, and that's when I notice he's naked—which makes sense since he's getting in the shower with me. His dick is semi-hard, and it bobs heavy between his thighs as he steps toward me. The shower is a decent size, but not huge, so he doesn't have far to go. Wordlessly, Jase picks me up and pushes me against the wall. The water continues to fall around us, but it doesn't deter him in the slightest. My legs wrap around his waist, and my fingers grip his shoulders. His mouth finds mine, and he devours me. His tongue pushes through my lips, and I taste everything that is Jase. His cock pokes against my ass, and I let out a moan, needing him to be inside me. The air around us grows thick with lust. Our bodies go from zero to one hundred in a split second, with a single touch. And a million thoughts hit me at once, like how is it so easy to get lost in this man? Is it like this for everyone in the beginning? Will it always feel this way with Jase? This explosive? Is this how it was for my mom?

My heart constricts as Jase pushes up into me, filling me completely. Our kiss turns rougher, more demanding. I can feel him everywhere. His fingers digging into my ass, his mouth devouring mine. His dick thrusting in and out of me. Every part of him is touching me. It's as if he's become an extension of me. He's gotten under my skin, and there's no getting him out.

The thought of leaving him has my throat tightening. Tears of devastation leak from my eyes. My arms wrap tightly around Jase's neck, needing to mold myself to him— to feel him even closer. I want to burrow myself just as deeply in him as he's done to me. My tears fall as Jase makes love to me against the shower wall. As reality hits that I can't leave this man. I am falling in love with him. I don't care if it's too soon, too fast. I can't help how my heart feels. I need to lay my cards down, put it all on the line—tell him the truth and see where it takes us. Maybe I can convince him to join me in New York. He could work at a shop there and eventually open his own place. Would his sister and brother be willing to move? Would he move without them? Am I crazy for even having these thoughts?

"Celeste," Jase moans, "stay with me, baby." His words push all my thoughts aside, so I can focus completely on being right here, in this moment, with Jase—on how good he feels inside me. His face nuzzles into the crook of my neck, and he bites down on my flesh as he comes deep inside me. Once he catches his breath, he lifts his head, pulls out of me, then sets me down on my feet.

"You didn't come," he says with a frown. It's not a question, he knows I didn't. We've only had sex a couple times, but every time he's made sure I find my release before him.

"I'm sorry," I whisper in embarrassment. I was so lost in myself, in him, I didn't even notice.

"What's going on?" He runs two fingers down the side of my cheek.

"Nothing." I shake my head. "Was everything okay with your friend?"

Jase's brows furrow. "Is that what's wrong? You have nothing to worry about. Amaya is only a friend."

"I know." I nod emphatically. I wait for Jase to further explain himself, but he doesn't.

"Hurry up and finish rinsing off," Jase says. "I owe you an orgasm." He shoots me an adorable wink before stepping out of the shower.

Continue reading about
Jase and Celeste in *On The Surface.*

Through His Eyes

Chapter One

QUINN

Sitting on my terrace, in a comfy lounge chair I purchased when Rick first bought us this place, I hold a glass of red wine in my hand—one that I have yet to take a sip of. I want to. I look forward to my nightly glass of wine. I buy my favorite brand in bulk and have it delivered to the condo. But for the last several weeks, I haven't been able to drink it. I still pour it and bring it out here like I've been doing every night for the last four years. Only, once I go back inside, I pour the crimson liquid down the sink and rinse the glass out. I think, somewhere deep in my subconscious, I believe that if I continue to pour it every night, eventually I'll be able to drink it. I've put it in my head that if I pretend like my life isn't about to change—well, technically, *already* has changed—then it won't. As if I can will my life to go back to what it was only a few short months ago. And that says a lot since I hated my life the way it was.

Drinking my nightly wine isn't just about drinking, though. It's about finding comfort in my nightly routine. It makes me feel like I have the tiniest semblance of control in a situation that, in reality, is completely out of my control. I can handle my current life. I know what to expect. It's routine and dependable. Rinse. Wash. Repeat. Now, though, not being able to drink wine means my routine is about to be shaken up, and I'm scared of what the future holds. It's easier to fight the monster you know than to take on the one you've never seen.

As I stare down at the hustle and bustle of the city, from the forty-seventh floor, I try to focus on what's in front of me and not what's inside of me. The problem is, from this high up, and this late at night, there's not really much of a view to focus on. Down below, I spot several flashes of lights from the cabs and bikes that make their way to their destinations. Tiny dots of people litter the sidewalks, but they're too small for me to see their features. I wonder how many of them are couples, holding hands and kissing, in love. My heart knots at the thought, and without thinking, I bring the wine to my lips. The liquid has only barely wet my tongue before I'm spitting it back into the glass and setting it down.

My eyes glide upward. The sky is clear tonight, so it should be filled with beautiful stars twinkling above. But with the bright lights that make up New York City, it's difficult to spot a single star. What I would give to be back in Piermont, in my old apartment in North Carolina that I shared with my brothers, staring up at the sky and counting the hundreds of stars that wink down at me.

My cell phone vibrates on the table. When I see it's my sister-in-law, Celeste, I hit ignore. I've been pushing everyone away for years. I know I have. But I don't know what to do, how to handle the situation I've found myself in. Once upon a time, I dreamt of being right here, in this moment: married to the love of my life, living in the most beautiful city in the world, in a gorgeous home. Pregnant with my husband's baby. Looking toward our future. How ironic is it that when my dreams finally come true, nothing is the way it's supposed to be.

I'm married, but my husband doesn't love me—and if I'm honest, I don't love him either. How do you love a man who hates every part of you? It's hard, trust me, I've tried. Over and over again. And through trying, I've lost a large piece of myself that I'm not sure I'll ever be able to find. When I look into the mirror, I'm not even sure who I see anymore, and that scares the crap out of me, because I wasn't always this way. I was strong and determined and full of life, and now...I'm not. I'm weak, and I hate that I know it, yet choose not to do anything about it. It makes me feel even weaker.

I might live in a beautiful city, but it's one I no longer get to experience because I'm stuck in this suffocating ivory tower, going through the motions but not actually living. Where I live is beautiful. The furniture, the paintings, everything expensive and top of the line, but it's not a home. It's simply a dwelling. A place to eat and sleep. And I can't imagine what it will feel like to raise a baby here.

Rick and I tried for years to get pregnant. He wanted a baby with his last name, and I wanted someone to love. After four years of trying, at thirty-four years old, I didn't think it would happen. I brought up the idea of using in vitro fertilization a couple years back, but my husband scoffed at me and told me he's not defective, and only defective people need to use IVF. Then, he proceeded to tell me I was probably the defective one, and if that were the case, he didn't want a baby with me anyway. I swallow thickly at the memory of crying myself to sleep that night. My eyes burn, and I close them tight, willing the tears to vaporize. Rick doesn't deserve any more of my tears. I know that. But, still, they come. Because I'm weak.

Glancing at the time on my cell phone, I see it's almost ten o'clock. Rick should be home soon. I'm planning to tell him about the baby tonight. I'm not naïve enough to believe that a baby will repair our marriage, but I don't know what else to do. It's not as if things can get worse. My thoughts go back to when I was a little girl. Of my father and mother yelling and screaming at each other. Of my mother hitting him and calling him names. Of the way she turned her hatred onto me when he died from a heart attack, and she found out the extent of his cheating. I was only eight years old, but I can still remember the way my brothers tried to protect me. I know they would protect me now, if they knew, if I let them in.

I pick up my glass of wine, and once again, have to stop myself from downing the entire glass. Closing my lids, I try to imagine how my baby's life will look. I refuse to let him, or her, grow up like I did. Scared to talk out of turn, frightened of what mood my mother would be in when I got home from school. Terrified, that the nasty words she spoke about me were true.

It wasn't until my eldest brother, Jax, turned eighteen and gained guardianship of me, that I was finally able to breathe. At the same time, my other older brother Jase became emancipated. From the time I was eleven years old, I grew up in a loving home. I was given everything I could want or need. They treated me like a princess, and when I grew up, all I wanted was to meet a man who would treat me like his queen. Boy, was I naïve. Fairytales are overrated if you ask me. Maybe the problem was that every girl wants a Prince Charming, and I got a king. One who rules with an iron fist to keep his castle in order. He's well-respected by everyone and answers to no one. Maybe what I should've looked for, instead, was a sweet prince, one who would find my glass slipper, or show me a beautiful library. He would kiss me awake to save me from the evil witch, or take me away from the horrendous stepmother. Maybe the problem was that, because my brothers told me I deserved the world, when I wished upon those shooting stars, I aimed too high. You know what they say: *be careful what you wish for because you just might get it.* Well, I wished and wished and wished, and I got it...and now I have no damn clue what to do with it.

Glancing over at my phone, I notice five more minutes have passed. It's time to go inside. I need to clean the kitchen and put Rick's dinner out for him. He texted me earlier that he would be home at ten. After rinsing out my wine glass, I take his dinner out of the warmer and place it on the table for him along with some silverware and the scotch he always has with his dinner. Then I head into the bathroom to freshen up. Using a makeup wipe, I swipe under my eyes so the black is no longer smeared, and I no longer look like a racoon. When I reach into my drawer to grab a night shirt, I spot the lingerie I bought while out shopping with Celeste a while back. I was hoping to spice up my marriage, only when I put it on, Rick told me I looked like a trashy hooker and demanded I take it off. I'm not even sure why I kept it.

Instead of grabbing my cotton shirt, I pull out the silk, beige negligée that Rick bought me for our honeymoon, from out of the bottom of the drawer. It's on the shorter side, touching just above the top of my knees, and is thin, showing all of my curves that Rick used to love but now despises. Taking a deep breath, I throw it on. It's probably a stupid idea, but I'm desperate—for affection, for attention, for any sign that my marriage isn't completely over. Maybe the sight of this negligée will remind him of a time when he actually found me attractive, and he'll go back to being the man I first met. The man I gave my heart to. The man I wanted so desperately to have a family with.

When I hear the door alarm chime, indicating Rick is home, I rush out to greet him. He's toeing off his expensive loafers and shrugging out of his suit jacket, when I make my presence known. He looks up, and I hold my breath, praying his reaction will be receptive. That he'll once again look at me like I'm his entire world. He'll take me into his arms and lay me down on the bed and make love to me. I'll tell him about the baby, and he'll spend the rest of the night worshipping my body.

I'll be the respected queen to my king.

For a brief moment, he stares at me. His gaze rakes down my body, and I think maybe today will be different. But then his face contorts into his usual look of disgust, and I know whatever he's about to say won't be good. So I do what I have learned to do over the years—put up my broken and fragile wall and pray his harsh words aren't strong enough this time to completely demolish it.

"You would think with all the time on your hands, you would make an effort to lose weight," he quips. "What else do you do all day?" He shoots me an accusatory look that makes me want to tell him to go fuck himself. And that makes me a bit proud that I still have even a single ounce of strength left in me to consider saying it. Even though it does no good when I don't actually have any intention of acting on it. Been there, done that. Not stupid enough to ever do it again.

Instead, I stay stuck in my place as if my feet are glued to the ground beneath me—my voice refusing to speak the words I so badly want to say. I'm well aware I don't do shit all day because he gives me a hard time every time I leave—always pointing out a woman's place is in the home.

After the first few times of Rick putting me down, I started to go to the gym in our building, only he showed up and caused a scene when he saw me talking to one of the men who worked out there. It didn't matter that he was only showing me how to properly use one of the machines. He forbade me to ever return, telling me I could workout at home. Months went by, and he kept pointing out I was putting on weight. He then began to put me down during sex, making comments about everything I ate, and pointing out the type of woman he *does* find attractive. At that point, I met with a nutritionist, who mentioned that stress can cause weight gain. It doesn't help that I'm an emotional eater, and dealing with my husband can be emotionally stressful. I try to eat healthy, but it doesn't matter because I'm not what he wants, and I never will be.

Whenever I would go to Forbidden Ink, my brothers' tattoo shop, to hang out, he would give me a hard time, saying it's not appropriate. When I would try to hang out with my sister-in-law, Celeste, and my niece Skyla, he would come up with a list of items that needed to be done. I still make it a point to see them when Rick goes away, but the more unhappy I become, the more my family notices, and the less I bring myself around them, not wanting to have to explain that my entire life is a lie and in shambles.

Setting his jacket on the table, Rick steps closer and takes the silky fabric of the negligée between his fingers. "Delicate items like these are meant for women who take care of their bodies, not for women who let their bodies go to shit. Take it off. *Now.* You don't deserve to wear something so exquisite when you clearly don't appreciate it."

Knowing better than to respond, I nod once and turn on my heel. I knew this was going to happen, so why would I willingly put myself in this situation? Maybe I just needed to hear it one last time. For him to confirm where we stand.

"Wait," he says, and I turn around, my heart filling with false hope. "Put my shoes and jacket away," he commands, his voice devoid of all emotion.

I nod again, walking over to grab his jacket, and then reaching down to grab his shoes. When I stand upright, I feel his hand on my wrist. I look up into his cold, blue eyes. The same eyes I once found warmth in. "How do you think it makes me feel as your husband, to have to see the way you've let yourself go? I'm the one who has to see you naked...touch you...How can you expect me to want you when you don't care about your own body?"

"I'm sorry," I murmur softly, unsure of what else to say. The truth of the matter is, I've only gained about twenty-five pounds since we've gotten together, but it's enough that my husband no longer views me as attractive. I've always been on the thicker side: wide hips, thick thighs, big breasts. I was never the most popular or the prettiest, but I was okay with who I was. Until Rick made sure to point out every flaw. Every imperfection. Day after day he broke me piece by piece. I don't know how I even let it go on this long.

But, I finally did reach my breaking point and made the decision to leave—to go to my brothers and tell them everything. I formulated a plan to move out and file for divorce. I knew Rick would give me shit, but it couldn't be any worse than living under his roof. But fate is a fickle bitch and the day I was going to meet with my brothers, I realized I missed my period. I waited and waited, but it never came. Now, three months later and I still haven't gotten it. I've yet to take a test, but I know what the results will say. I'm pregnant by a man who hates me.

Rick's brows dip together at my apology—in confusion or frustration, I'm not sure—and I wonder, maybe, if I'd worked out harder, dieted more seriously, my husband would want and love me. It's too late now, though. Pregnant women only get fatter. I've already started to put weight on, and my body is already changing. My clothes are becoming tighter. What will he think of me once I'm fully showing? Will he despise our baby for doing this to my body, like he despises me for letting myself go? No, he's wanted an *heir* for too long. I refuse to believe he won't love our child. *But does he even know how to love?*

My thoughts and feelings are scattered all over the place. I'm a mess of hormones. Getting pregnant was what I wanted for so long, but now that it's happened, I can't help but wish it wouldn't have. I feel a tremendous amount of guilt for even thinking that, but the last thing I want is to bring a baby into this unloving home. I was raised in one for years before Jax saved me, and I wouldn't wish that on anyone, especially my own child. Even if Rick, by some crazy chance, loves our child the way a father should love his baby, he, or she, will still grow up watching him treat me like shit—the same way I watched my parents treat each other. Will my child resent me for being weak, or will he, or she, view me the same way Rick does? The thought has me wanting to throw up.

As I scurry back to the room, I try to recall when Rick changed. You hear about it in books and movies. They talk about it on those shows like Dr. Phil or Oprah. The woman who lives in the abusive household. How does she not notice? Why doesn't she leave? She must be blind, deaf, and dumb not to see the signs. All I can say is, until you are standing where I am, you won't understand. Words can hit as hard as fists. Without even realizing I was standing in the ring, being thrown into a fight I wasn't ready for, I had already been knocked to the ground. Did I get up? Of course. But when you get knocked down so many times, eventually you realize it's better to just tap out. I'm aware it makes me sound weak. But in my defense, the fight isn't even close to being fair. I never really stood a chance.

I can still remember the days when Rick would kiss me lovingly. The way he would hold me in his arms and tell me how much I meant to him. I can't pinpoint the moment when things changed. When we went from having sex every day, to a few days a week, down to once a week, and eventually it turned into once a month. When our weekly date nights turned into me leaving dinner out for him. And our weekend getaways turned into Rick going away by himself while I stayed home alone.

I kept telling myself we were just in a rut. His job is stressful. His father puts a lot of pressure on his shoulders. But at some point, I realized it was me. In my husband's eyes, I was no longer beautiful. No longer attractive. I didn't make him smile or laugh anymore. I didn't turn him on. He saw me as a burden, a nuisance. I was no longer his queen who was meant to stand by his side. Instead, I became a prisoner he kept holed up in this condo, waiting in the background to be at his disposal. I once was building a successful photography company, but he demanded I stay home. He said it would be an embarrassment for his wife to be working. We were trying to have a baby, and he told me he wanted me to be a stay-at-home mom just like his mother was. If I were working, people would think he couldn't take care of what was his. He cared more about the outward appearance than what was actually happening in our home.

I place Rick's shoes neatly on his shoe rack, then grab a hanger to hang up his jacket. As I'm shaking out the material to ensure there are no wrinkles, I catch a whiff of perfume. Bringing my nostrils to the lapels, I inhale deeply and confirm it. His jacket smells like a woman. My stomach roils in disgust. My hands begin to tremble in fury. My husband is having an affair. I am now *officially* the cliché.

The thought of him cheating on me sparks something inside me. I've given up everything for this man. Meanwhile, he's out screwing another woman. I don't doubt she's gorgeous. She's probably a size one with perky breasts, silky blond hair, and has flawless skin with zero tattoos—pretty much the exact opposite of my black, lifeless hair, dull black eyes, and tattoo-covered overweight body.

Peering out of the room, I see he's sitting at the dining room table, eating his dinner and texting on his phone. And a plan surfaces. Changing into a pair of sweats and a tee, I go pee and then lay down in bed, closing my eyes and pretending to fall asleep. As I wait for Rick to finish eating, I think about the woman's scent on his jacket. This isn't the first time I've spelled woman's perfume on his clothes, but I chose to remain in denial, making excuses— he was probably standing too close to his secretary, or he had lunch with his mom. I didn't want to admit that my husband was having an affair. But deep down I always knew. It's only now, that I'm pregnant and carrying an innocent precious baby in me, that I'm finally opening my eyes and looking around me.

A little while later, Rick enters our room without saying a word. I hear the bathroom door shut, and I jump out of bed. He takes a shower every night when he gets home, after dinner, and he always brings his cell phone into the bathroom with him. Because of the bathroom being so big, he can't see me enter, but the door creaks, and he calls out, "Quinn?"

"Sorry," I say, "I need to go pee. I'll be right out." When I don't hear him respond, I peek around the corner and see him standing in the shower under the water.

Cheater. Asshole. Homewrecker.

Snatching his phone out of his pants that he has folded on the vanity, I type in his passcode and pull up his messages. I click on the first one: Sylvia. The name sounds familiar. I think she's his secretary. Just as I'm about to click out and go to the next one, I spot their most recent thread.

SYLVIA

I miss you already.

RICK

I'll take you out tomorrow night. Send me a picture.

SYLVIA

<insert topless image>

Of course, he's cheating on me with his damn secretary. Because my entire story wasn't cliché enough, it had to add the young, hot blond with huge, fake breasts. I skim through a couple more texts before I get nervous of being caught. I'm not sure why I even care. Our marriage is obviously over, but something in me screams that I need to tread lightly. It's no longer just me. I now have my baby that I need to protect. Screenshotting the messages, I text them to my phone and then send Sylvia's contact information to myself as well. I quickly scroll through Rick's other messages and find several other women he's been messaging with. I send all of their info to myself, then delete all the evidence that I was ever on his phone. Exiting out of his apps, I lock his screen and put his phone back where he left it, tiptoeing out of the bathroom and climbing back into bed. Putting my phone on silent, I store it in my nightstand drawer, so he won't see it, just in case.

When he gets out of the shower, he walks over to the dresser with a towel wrapped around his waist. I take a second to check him out. He's not fat like I am...he's skinny. Not toned or muscular, but thin and lanky. His skin is tanned, not a tattoo in sight. His brown hair is wet and combed over, and his face is clean-shaven. He's a good-looking guy, but he isn't like *Wow*. His looks aren't what attracted me to him, though. It was his charm and self-confidence. He was so sure of himself, sure of his place in the world, and even though I came across like I was just as strong and confident, I felt lost. I thought when he found me, I would feel like I finally belonged, and I did... until he decided I was no longer what he wanted, and he left me alone once again. Now I'm more lost than I was before, and my only hope is that I somehow find my way on my own.

"What are your plans this weekend?" he asks, not looking at me as he drops his towel and pulls his boxers up his legs.

"Celeste is throwing Sky a birthday party at their place. She's turning eighteen." Skyla is my niece—Jase and Celeste's daughter. When she was younger, before Jase and Celeste got together, we were close. Helping Jase to raise her is what made me realize I wanted my own family. I wanted someone to love and to love me back. I wanted to feel wanted and needed. Once Jase and Celeste got together, Skyla and Celeste hit it off straight away. They're like two peas in a pod. I'm glad Skyla has a fulltime mother-figure in her life, but I can't help but wish that I had the bond they share. Maybe one day I'll have the kind of relationship they have, with my son or daughter.

"I have to work, so I won't be able to go." I don't know why he's letting me know this. He never comes to any of my family functions anymore.

"Okay, will I see you at home afterward?"

He stills in his place for a split-second, and if I wasn't looking for it, I wouldn't have noticed. But now my eyes are wide open, and I'm definitely looking. "Probably not," he says. "I have a late meeting." He clears his throat then continues. "I might not make it home. I'll probably just stay at the office."

Liar. Cheater. Asshole.

"But tomorrow is the weekend," I push. I never push. I never question. I just accept. And I hate that I've become that woman who just accepts. "Why would you spend the night when it will be Sunday? You don't work on Sunday...I was thinking we could go to the farmer's market like we used to. Pick up some fresh fruits and vegetables." When we first got together, we used to go to the farmer's market every Sunday. We would check out each booth, hand in hand, laughing and talking about our week. Even when he was busy, he would make sure he left Sundays open for us.

"Maybe next weekend," he says, his eyes meeting mine through his reflection in the mirror. "This meeting is too important." And it's in this moment that I know without a doubt my husband cheating on me isn't something new. His flat tone and blank expression are identical to the ones he's been giving me for too long. Of course, I couldn't have dug my head out of the sand before I got pregnant by my lying, cheating husband. And of course, after years of trying, and failing, we were successful the one time he came home sloppy drunk and actually wanted me—only to wake up the next morning and not even remember it.

He pulls his shirt over his head and says, "I have work to do. Goodnight," then leaves the room as quickly as he came.

Chapter Two

QUINN

I'M SITTING IN THE BACKYARD OF MY BROTHER and Celeste's home, at Skyla's birthday party, watching everyone's kids run around and play. The laughter that fills the air should have my heart swelling with love, but instead, it fills me with dread. I was going to tell Rick this morning that I'm pregnant, but when I woke up, he was already gone. No note, no kiss goodbye, not even a text message. Some would say I'm crazy for telling him I'm pregnant. I should run as far away from him as possible, but I know better. This isn't some romance novel. I'm not going to escape and find myself some perfect single guy next door to fall in love with while I attempt to rebuild my shell of a life. This is real life, and in my reality, I have to deal with the cards I've been dealt. If I don't play nice, I know Rick will have no problem taking our baby away from me. He has more money than God, and I've seen the cruel and ruthless way he does business. There's a reason the companies he and his father run are so successful. My husband is a smart, conniving, businessman who never holds back. The last thing I need is for him to do what my father did to Jase and Jax's mom—prove me to be an unfit mom and take my baby from me.

I'm going to have to play nice. Let Rick take the lead. He's apparently busy screwing his way through New York, and as long as I continue to turn a blind eye, he will continue to do so while I raise our baby. His money will pay for everything materialistic our child needs, while my love will provide everything he, or she, emotionally needs. *That is if I can somehow keep him from putting me down in front of our child*...I will not allow my baby to suffer like I did. I won't argue with Rick. I won't fight against him. I won't let my baby become a pawn in this horrible game I'm being forced to play. I'll do my best to be the wife he wants me to be, so I can give my baby a stable and loving home.

I listen as Celeste and Jase's friends laugh and joke with one another. At one point, their friend Killian announces that he and his wife, Giselle, are expecting their second baby. Everyone congratulates them, and then Olivia, another friend of Celeste's, announces that she and her husband, Nick, are also expecting. It will be their third, and they are beyond ecstatic. Not able to take another second of being surrounded by all of these happy couples—knowing my husband is somewhere most likely fucking his secretary—I duck out quietly and head inside.

I'm not ready to go home yet, but I also don't want to be around people, so I slip into Celeste and Jase's bedroom, so I can use their bathroom without running into anyone.

I go pee, wash my hands, and then find myself sitting on the edge of the tub, unsure of where to go from here. What if I did run? What if I took whatever cash I could find and bought an old, used car to drive away from here? Would he search for me? Hell, he doesn't even like me. I don't understand why he even wants to keep me. He doesn't know I'm pregnant. If I ran away now, would he even think twice about me? I could send him divorce papers from wherever I end up and hope he signs them. I could raise my baby in a loving home by myself. But what if he comes after me? What if one day while I'm walking down the street, taking the baby for a walk, he finds me? He would take my baby. I know he would. He would make me regret leaving, every single day for the rest of my life.

I'm not even aware that I'm crying, until a soft voice interrupts my thoughts. "You okay?" I look up and see Celeste standing in front of me.

"I think I'm pregnant," I admit nervously.

"And that's a bad thing..." she says carefully. I hate that she treats me like I'm fragile, but it's my fault. Both my brothers are happy and in love, and I want what they have. I want to be in love, and being around them every day has become harder and harder. So I've just stopped coming around. It's easier this way.

Not knowing what to say to Celeste, I just shrug.

"Well, there's only one way to find out." She pulls a box of pregnancy tests out from under the counter.

"You keep tests on hand?" I ask, shocked.

"We've been trying for the last year," she admits. As she rips the test open, she tells me how difficult it's been for them. The first time they got pregnant, it happened rather quickly, and they had twin daughters, Mariah and Melina, who are now two years old.

She hands me a disposable cup to pee in, and I blurt out, "I'm sorry, Celeste. Here I am, unsure if I'm happy or sad that I'm most likely pregnant, and you're wishing for a baby."

"Everyone has their own stories," she says with a soft smile. "Take it, and I'll be right here with you."

A few minutes later, the test confirms what I already knew. I'm pregnant. Celeste, as if she knows exactly what I need in this moment, pulls me into a hug. "Jase and I will be here for you no matter what." Not wanting to lose it right here in her bathroom, I thank her and tell her I'm going to head home.

"Okay. If you need anything, call me."

When I get to my car—a Porsche Cayenne Rick bought me for my birthday a couple years ago—I lay my head against the steering wheel and let every emotion out that I've been holding in. As my chest racks with gut-wrenching sobs, I allow myself to mourn over the loss of myself, my future, the loving family I long for. With every tear that falls, I'm one step closer to accepting my fate. And when all my tears have released, and I'm incapable of shedding another drop of salty liquid, I turn my car on and drive home.

THE SOUND OF MY PHONE CONTINUOUSLY vibrating against the top of my nightstand wakes me from a restless sleep. I contemplated leaving Rick more than a hundred times last night. Packing up my stuff and taking off. But in order to do that, I need to plan, and by the time I figure it all out, I'll already be showing and he'll know I'm pregnant.

Reaching over, I grab the phone and press answer without even looking at who's calling. "Good evening, I'm calling from New York General Hospital. May I please speak to Quinn Thompson?" *New York General?*

"This is she," I say, sitting up slightly. Pulling the phone from my ear, I quickly check the time: two a.m.

"For security purposes, can you please confirm your current physical address and date of birth?" she asks.

After I raddle off my home address and date of birth, she thanks me and says, "You are listed as Richard Thompson's next of kin. We need you to come in, please."

My heart pounds against my ribcage and my breathing becomes labored—out of fear or hope, I haven't determined. "Did something happen to my husband?"

"Unfortunately, we can't give any information over the phone. We're going to need you to come in."

"Okay," I say, robotically standing and finding clothes to put on. I'm about to head to the hospital when Celeste's earlier words come back to me: *Jase and I will be here for you, no matter what...If you need anything, call me.* I don't know how, but something tells me I'm going to need my family.

Not wanting to wake up Celeste and Jase since they have two little ones, I dial my brother Jax's number. He answers on the first ring, his voice groggy from sleep.

"I need you," I whisper.

Twenty minutes later, he picks me up and we head over to the hospital. When I get to the front desk, I give the receptionist my husband's name, and she gives me directions on where to go. As we step around the corner, I spot her. Blond hair, petite body, perky, young breasts. Sylvia, my husband's secretary-slash-mistress is sitting on the couch of the waiting room, bawling her eyes out. I've seen her a few times when I visit Rick at work, but he's never formally introduced us. I only knew she was his secretary by her name because she always answers the phone when I call.

Averting my gaze, I walk straight over to the desk I was told to go to and give them Rick's name. The woman types on the keyboard for several seconds before her eyes meet mine and she gives me a look of sympathy mixed with sadness. "The police have requested to speak with you." She stands and walks me over to the two men in uniform. Both are standing in the corner, near the coffee machine, but only one is drinking a cup of coffee.

"This is Richard Thompson's wife," she says, and both men's eyes widen.

When neither of them say anything, Jax loses his patience. "Can someone please tell us what the hell is going on?"

"Yes, sir," the cop, who was just drinking the coffee, says. "We received a call tonight about a man who was held at gunpoint." My body begins to tremble as I take in the words he's saying.

Pulling me into his side, Jax asks, "What happened?"

"A homeless man, under the influence and armed with a stolen weapon, approached your husband when he was getting into his vehicle. According to the witness—"

"What witness?" I ask, already knowing the answer, but needing to hear him say it.

The cop without the coffee, frowns. "The woman who was walking with your husband to his vehicle."

"Who?" I push. My hands fist at my sides in frustration.

"We're not at liberty to say, as the case is still under investigation," the cop with the coffee says, but his eyes dart over to where Sylvia is sitting. I nod once to thank him, and he grants me a sad smile.

"I'm sorry, ma'am," the cop without the coffee says.

"According to the witness, your husband was asked for his wallet when they were coming out of the restaurant. Unaware the man had a gun, he told him no, and when he turned his back to get into his vehicle, he was shot from behind. The man took off, and the woman called nine-one-one. He was brought in, but didn't make it through surgery."

Jax's arm around me tightens, and when I look over, his gaze is flitting from the officers to Sylvia. He's putting the pieces together.

Liar. Cheater. Asshole.

"Did you catch the man who shot him?" I ask.

"We did. We found him shooting up on the corner. He wasn't even trying to hide. He's been arrested, and is being held, while we complete the investigation, but we wanted to be here to tell you what happened ourselves."

"Thank you," I tell the cops, fully aware that my voice isn't even cracking. This is the part where I'm supposed to cry. Even though my marriage was in shambles, and my husband hated me and was cheating on me, I should still feel something. Anything. I was with him for just over four years—married for almost three of them. Surely, that has to amount to at least a tear. But standing here, in the hallway of the hospital, I can't conjure up a single damn drop of moisture. Maybe it really is possible to run out of tears...

And then I hear sobs coming from behind me. I look back over at Sylvia. Her tiny body is shaking uncontrollably. *That should be me*, I tell myself. I should be the one crying like my life is over. I'm pregnant, and my husband is dead.

Before I can think about what I'm doing, I'm standing in front of Sylvia. She looks up, her perfect, flawless face, streaked with her makeup.

"You realize you're crying over a married man who you were having an affair with, right?" I say, my voice flat, devoid of all emotion. I hear several gasps, but I don't look anywhere but at Sylvia.

She wipes the snot from her nose and takes several deep breaths before she finally speaks. "You might've trapped him in a loveless marriage, but Rick loved me. He was trying to find a way to divorce you because he didn't love you. He didn't want you," she says, her voice getting louder with each word she speaks.

"Is that what he told you?" I ask, stifling the manic laugh I feel bubbling up inside of me. "That's a lie. He could've divorced me at any time he wanted. *Nothing* was keeping us together."

"He was afraid you would take all his money," she hisses. "He worked so hard and he knew you would try to take it all...because you're trash!"

"We have a prenup," I inform her, and her eyes go wide in shock. Yep, looks like he's been lying to you, too. "Did he mention that he was sleeping with several other women besides you?"

Sylvia glares and stands. "You're lying. You are a lying,

fat, needy bitch," she spits.

"Hey!" Jax booms, ready to defend his littler sister's honor, but I hold my hand up to stop him. I should be mad at this woman, but I'm not. Every time a man cheats on a woman, the mistress gets blamed. She's called a homewrecker, told she's destroyed their marriage. But the thing is, if a marriage is solid, there's no wrecking a home. There's no destroying a marriage. This woman was lied to, just like I was. Just like all the other women I'm sure were lied to. Sure, she knew Rick was married, but he's the one who made the vows, not her. And I can see it in her eyes, she loves my husband.

The only thing I feel is pity towards her.

Pulling out my phone, I select the screenshots I saved and send them to her. "Rick Thompson was a lying, cheating, selfish bastard," I tell her. "I've sent you the proof that he was sleeping with at least three other women aside from us that I know of. I wish you the best."

As I turn to walk away, Sylvia says, "Aside from us? That's how I know you're lying. Your husband wasn't sleeping with you. He could barely stand to look at you, let along fuck you." I consider pointing out that I'm pregnant just to spite her, but decide against it. It's none of her business.

"That's enough!" Jax roars. "Let's go, Quinn." Wrapping his arm around my shoulders, he walks me out of the hospital. When I ask him to please take me home, he refuses and brings me back to the townhouse in Cobble Hill, the one I was living in with him and Jase before I fell for Rick's charm and agreed to move in with him. Since then, Jase and Skyla have moved out and in with Celeste, and Willow, my brother's girlfriend, has moved in. When we get back to his place, Willow makes me a hot cup of tea, while Jax holds me until I fall asleep. I have no idea what I would do without my family.

Chapter Three

QUINN

I CONSIDERED GOING TO THE FUNERAL, IF FOR no other reason than to gain some closure. Jax insisted he and Willow would go with me so I wouldn't be forced to face Rick's parents on my own. The morning of, he came out of his room dressed in a suit, with his hair gelled neatly, and Willow came out looking gorgeous in a tight yet modest black dress. Jax drove over to the condo, and I picked out a black dress and heels, then showered and got dressed. But on the way, I told them I couldn't do it. I couldn't walk into that church and put on a fake front, playing the part of the heartbroken, mourning widow.

Especially after calling Rick's parents to tell them what happened, only to learn Sylvia was over and had already told them. Jacquelyn, Rick's mom, went on to say that she and Sylvia would handle the funeral. That she knows what her son would want, and Sylvia, the amazing secretary she is, would help organize everything. While

I should've been offended my husband's mistress was helping to plan his funeral, instead, I felt relief.

Kenneth, Rick's father, called me to let me know when and where the funeral would be held, and also to let me know the following day would be the reading of the will. While the thought of taking a single penny from my cheating husband made me sick, I now have a baby on the way, and I'll be damned if he, or she, will go without because of my stubbornness.

So, here I sit, in a chair in my father-in-law's office across from my mother-in-law, waiting for their attorney to begin the reading of the will. Jax, of course, offered to go with me, but I told him this was something I needed to do on my own. It's time I start standing on my own two feet again.

"Does anybody need anything? Water? Coffee?" I glance over and see Sylvia standing in the doorway. She's wearing a loose, almost see-through flowy blouse matched with a conservative pencil skirt. Her blond hair is neatly pulled back into a harsh bun, and her makeup is done to perfection. As she strides across the room, her tiny ass sways, and I briefly wonder, if I completely starve myself, could I ever be as small as she is? I can't even picture it.

When I don't answer her, Jacquelyn says, "Quinn, don't be rude. Sylvia is asking you a question."

"Excuse me?" I snap, wishing now that I would've let Jax accompany me.

"She asked you if you wanted something to drink. The

polite response would be yes, please or no, thank you." A very unladylike snort comes from me, and Jacquelyn's eyes widen. In all the years I've been with Rick, I've never shown any kind of disrespect to his parents. Without having any of my own, I was hoping to develop a relationship with Rick's. Unfortunately, I learned fairly quickly that the only people more cruel and cold than Rick, are his parents.

"Let me get this straight," I say. "You want me to be polite to the woman who was fucking my husband for the last several months, maybe even years. The woman, who was with him the night he died because instead of being with his wife at a family get together, he was taking his mistress out to dinner with the plan to fuck her afterward." Jaquelyn gasps, Sylvia sniffles, and Kenneth glares. And I take a deep, cleansing breath because holy shit, it felt good to speak my mind and stand up for myself.

"Oh, you didn't know? That your son was a lying, cheating, piece of shit? And spoiler alert." I take a moment to look at each of them before I continue. "She wasn't the only one. There were several."

"How dare you!" Jacquelyn yells. "My son is dead! Don't you dare spread lies about him. You will not tarnish his reputation." Of course her only concern is his reputation.

Before I can respond, the family attorney walks in. Needing to keep up their appearances, Jacquelyn and Kenneth both compose themselves and greet Mr. Levine.

Sylvia asks if he would like anything, and when he says no, she scurries out.

The will is read. Due to the prenuptial agreement I signed, and the fact that we were only married for three years, everything that is related to the company goes to his father since they are partners. Rick left me the condo, since he paid it off and put my name on the deed as a wedding gift. The Porsche is also mine, as well as whatever is in our joint checking account where he used to deposit my "allowance" as he liked to call it. His sole bank accounts apparently go to his father, as it states in the will, to be used for the business. I am the sole beneficiary of the life insurance policy he took out on himself after we were married, though, so there's that. Mr. Levine hands me all of the paperwork, and when I look at it, I see the policy is worth a million dollars. Outwardly, I don't show any emotion, but inwardly, I'm breathing a sigh of relief that I'll have the means to take care of my baby.

After thanking him, and without saying goodbye to my in-laws, because good fucking riddance, I walk out of the door and out of the building for the last time. Of course, Jax is waiting outside for me.

"You okay?" he asks, walking with me.

"I will be," I tell him truthfully. When we get to my car, he takes my keys from me so he can drive.

"What's next?"

"I was thinking I would put the condo up for sale. I don't want to live there anymore," I admit, instinctually placing a hand over my belly. I can't imagine raising my baby in the same home where Rick would tear me down and belittle me on a daily basis. I need a fresh start. I can't change the past, nor would I want to, since it gave me the precious baby in my belly, but I can sure as hell control my future.

Jax notices my hand and asks, "Is it true?" He nods toward my belly. "Are you pregnant?"

"Did Celeste tell you?"

"No, she wouldn't say anything, but Jase hinted at it."

"Yeah, I am, which is why I want to move. I need a fresh start."

"You know, there's a perfectly decent-size townhouse with two out of the three rooms available." He smiles softly at me, and for the first time in a long time, my heart feels content. "And I heard it's a great place to raise a baby until you're ready to get back on your feet again." He's referring to Jase raising Skyla there until she was thirteen and they moved out to start their life with Celeste.

"Are you sure?" I ask. "I don't want to impose on you and Willow." Jax and Willow have been together for almost as long as Rick and me, but I've never once heard them discuss having babies or getting married. I can't imagine a couple with no kids would want their home to be overtaken by a single mom and her baby.

Jax grins. "I'm more than sure. It was actually Willow's idea."

"Can I ask you a question?" I don't want to get in

their business, but I've always wondered…He nods once. "Is there a reason Willow and you haven't gotten married or had any kids?"

Jax's smile drops, and I worry I've overstepped. I've always had a close relationship with my brothers—sharing a home with them for the first thirty years of my life will do that. But over the last four years, since I got together with Rick and my life slowly began to spiral out of control, our relationship has deteriorated. Now, I fear, I may never be able to repair the damage that's been done.

"I don't usually like to share someone else's story, but Willow already told me that if the time ever came when I was in a situation where I needed to explain, I could." He scrubs his hands over his face before he looks back at me. "Willow was diagnosed with endometrial cancer at a young age. It required a full hysterectomy."

I gasp at his words. Poor Willow. I was over here feeling sorry for myself for getting pregnant by my asshole, cheating husband, meanwhile, she can never have a baby of her own. "I'm so sorry, Jax." I lay my hand on his arm. "Are you…" I feel bad even asking this, but I have to. He's my brother. "Are you okay with not having kids?"

Jax smiles and nods. "I am. I love Willow. I offered to adopt with her a few times, but she's said no every time. I think by getting cancer so young, it made her realize how short life can be. So instead of dwelling on what she can't have, she focuses on what she does have. And we're blessed with all our nieces from Jase and Celeste, and soon we'll have one from you. Who knows? Maybe you'll be the one to finally give everyone a damn nephew." We both laugh, and it feels good. It feels right.

"Seriously, though," he says with hearts in his eyes, "Willow is my other half. She's all I need to spend the rest of my life a happy man." I swoon over his admittance. Why couldn't I have found a guy more like my brothers?

"Well, if you guys are sure, then I'm there. But if, at any time, you guys want your privacy back, please just tell me. I'm not broke," I tell him. "I received money in Rick's will that will take care of my baby and me."

"Good," Jax says, "it's the least the asshole could do after what he put you through."

After we pack up a suitcase of my clothes, Jax tells me he'll have a moving company handle the rest. I let him know I don't want any of the furniture and it can be sold with the place. Anything that's Rick's, his parents can have, and whatever they don't take, can be donated to charity. He says he'll handle it all.

When we pull up to the townhouse, I spot Celeste's SUV in the driveway, and Jax says, "Celeste thought it was a nice day for a family barbeque. If you're not up for it..."

"No." I shake my head. "That actually sounds pretty damn perfect."

We walk inside, and I'm immediately greeted by Celeste, Jase, Willow, and Skyla. Everyone takes turns hugging me, and Willow even welcomes me home. Then, my two adorable nieces, in their little black pigtails and frilly matching dresses, come running over.

"Card for Auntie Quinn," Melina says, handing me a scribbled on, folded piece of paper.

"Love you," Mariah adds.

Bending down to their level, I scoop them both up into a hug, taking a moment to breathe them in and get lost in their innocence. In a few months I'm going to have one of my own. My own baby to love and spoil. The thought brings me to tears.

"Skyla, would you mind taking the girls out back to play for a few minutes?" Jase suggests, confusing my happy tears for sad ones.

"It's okay," I tell him. "I'm okay." I wait until the three girls are out of the room before I continue. "I was just thinking that in a few months I'm going to be a mom." My sobs get harder as I admit the truth to my family for the first time. "He was so mean, and I was so weak." I shake my head. "He would call me names and tell me I'm fat and should lose weight. And instead of leaving, I joined the gym. But then he accused me of cheating and forced me to quit." Tears fly down my face as I rush to get everything out.

"And he wouldn't let me work. I told you guys I didn't want to continue my photography business, but I was lying. He wouldn't let me. He gave me an allowance. A fucking allowance." I choke on my sobs. It feels almost cathartic to finally tell my family everything. "He would only have sex with me when he was drunk. He was cheating on me with God knows how many women." I bury my face in my hands, completely embarrassed, but Willow pulls them away.

"Don't do that," she demands. "Don't you hide. You have nothing to be embarrassed of."

"I'm okay," I repeat my earlier words. "Even though my husband was a horrible, despicable person, before he died he gave me the most precious gift." I cover my belly with my hands. "I was scared to admit I was pregnant. Terrified what my life would look like raising a baby with him. I thought about running away and never looking back. But he's dead." I smile because I'm finally free. "And I'm going to love my baby with everything in me. I'm going to be the best damn mother I can be."

Celeste and Willow both smile back, Jase looks like if Rick were still alive, he would find him and murder him, and Jax looks at me with brotherly love.

"So, where do you go from here?" Celeste asks. "What can we do?"

"First things first, I'm changing my last name back to Crawford, and then I'm going to take it one day at a time. It's time I finally find myself."

"And we'll be here for you every step of the way," Jase says, "just like you were there for me while I was trying to figure out how to raise Sky, how to navigate being a single dad." Jase pulls me into his arms for a hug. "We're family, Quinn. Let us be there for you, please."

Continue reading about
Lachlan and Quinn in *Through His Eyes*

About the Author

Reading is like breathing in, writing is like breathing out. – Pam Allyn

Nikki Ash resides in South Florida where she is an English teacher by day and a writer by night. When she's not writing, you can find her with a book in her hand. From the Boxcar Children, to Wuthering Heights, to the latest single parent romance, she has lived and breathed every type of book. While reading and writing are her passions, her two children are her entire world. You can probably find them at a Disney park before you would find them at home on the weekends!

Made in the USA
Coppell, TX
11 September 2024